Hard to Be Good

By Laura Kaye

Hard to Be Good

A HARD INK NOVELLA

LAURA KAYE

AVONIMPULSE
An Imprint of HarperCollinsPublishers

This is a work of fiction. Names, characters, places, and incidents are products of the author's imagination or are used fictitiously and are not to be construed as real. Any resemblance to actual events, locales, organizations, or persons, living or dead, is entirely coincidental.

Excerpt from *Hard to Let Go* copyright © 2015 by Laura Kaye.

EPub Edition APRIL 2015 ISBN: 9780062369499
Print Edition ISBN: 9780062369512

10 9 8 7 6 5 4 3

To Amanda for saying yes to J & C
To Christi for saying yowza!
And to the readers for loving Jeremy. For real, y'all!

Love knows no distinctions,
it only knows the joy of finding in another
everything your soul needs to feel complete.

Chapter 1

JEREMY RIXEY STOOD in front of the ruins of half of the warehouse building he owned in east Baltimore—his home for the past four years, and wondered what the hell had happened to his life.

As he carefully climbed up the pile of rubble, he didn't blame his older brother Nick or the other guys from Nick's former Army Special Forces team for what had happened. Not for his building being bombed by their enemies in the predawn hours the morning before, not for his tattoo shop being forced to close until the team's investigation finally ended, and not for turning his home into a boardinghouse for the team, their girlfriends, and the new allies they'd found in the Raven Riders Motorcycle Club.

No. Jeremy didn't blame Nick for the conspiracy and chaos that whirled all around them.

Because Jeremy felt like ten kinds of hell for not being able to do more to help Nick in the fight. A fight that went all the way back to Afghanistan, where the same assholes that attacked his building had also ambushed Nick's team, injuring Nick, killing seven others, and ultimately getting Nick and the other four survivors—Shane McCallan, Edward "Easy" Cantrell, Derek "Marz" DiMarzio, and Beckett Murda—kicked out of the Army.

Actually, it was worse than not being able to help. Jeremy was a damn liability.

Stepping from the pile of broken bricks, crumbled concrete, and twisted steel onto what was left of the exposed second floor, Jeremy dug his hands into his hair and tilted his head back, his gaze dragging up to the gray early-morning sky visible through the ruined roof another story above. Nick and everyone else were inside celebrating the decryption of a microchip full of information critical to their investigation, but Jeremy just couldn't put on a happy face right now.

Instead, his stomach plummeted as blurred memories sucked him back to the previous morning. Being awakened by gunfire. Nick asking if Jeremy was up to helping defend them. Running to the roof and exchanging fire with the thugs shooting from three black Suburbans down on the street. The thunderous impact of an explosive hitting the building.

And then all hell had really broken loose.

For a long moment, nothing seemed to happen, and then the roof had collapsed right underneath Jeremy. One minute there had been four stories of solid, hundred-year-old warehouse beneath his feet. The next . . . he was just falling.

Charlie had dived out of harm's way, but Jeremy had frozen. Full-on deer-in-the-headlights. His brain hadn't even registered what was happening before a painful clamp around his wrist hauled him back to safety. Nick had saved him. And because Jeremy had *needed* to be saved, two members of the Ravens that had been up there with them—men whom Nick had been standing closer to—had fallen to their deaths and died, one because he hadn't been able to hang on to the broken piece of rebar he'd managed to grab before Nick could get to him.

Jeremy would've liked to have thought that, in a crisis, he'd come through. But he hadn't. And men had died.

That was on Jeremy's shoulders. And the weight of it was so great he could barely keep from falling to his knees.

A tumble of bricks behind him.

Jeremy turned to see Charlie Merritt slowly making his way up.

The sight of the blond-haired man shot twin reactions through Jeremy's veins. Concern, because Charlie was already injured. Two of his fingers had been amputated by kidnappers just two weeks before. And relief, because Charlie always had this aura of quiet around him that was so peaceful it calmed all the shit whirling inside Jer's head. Which was really frickin' ironic since Charlie was the kidnapping victim who'd just learned that his army-colonel father had been murdered in Afghanistan.

"I knew I'd find you out here," Charlie said in that quiet way he had, his deep blue eyes trained on his footing.

"Yeah? Why's that?" Jeremy asked as he extended a

hand. Charlie grasped it as he made the last big step to the second floor. The touch was filled with the slow burn of attraction that Jeremy had felt toward the other man since they'd met after his rescue.

Charlie's eyes met Jeremy's, penetrating and intense, like he could read every thought Jeremy left unsaid. "Because I know this is hurting you." The words were spoken so quietly that the warm May wind whistling through the ruins nearly swallowed them, but they still hit Jeremy's chest like a thunderous clap.

All his life, Jeremy had been the one able to let almost everything roll right off his back. The one always cutting it up and laughing. The one who didn't care what people said about his facial piercings or the ink that covered him from neck to toes or even his bisexuality. Hell, he stood here in a shirt that read, *I'm trying to give up SEXUAL INNUENDOS. But it's hard . . . SO HARD!* But knowing he was responsible for the deaths of two men made him want to claw off his skin.

The backs of his eyes stinging, Jeremy turned away. He'd lost it once in front of Charlie. Yesterday. After the full weight of the attack had hit him. Last thing he wanted was to do it again. Because crying was so damn attractive. "All this can be fixed," he managed, waving vaguely at their surroundings.

"Don't do that," Charlie said, his sneakers scuffing against the thin layer of debris that littered the concrete floor.

Jeremy crossed the room to the remains of a window. It overlooked Hard Ink's giant, gravel-covered parking lot filled with the team's cars and trucks and the black-and-chrome gleam of over a dozen motorcycles. He braced a hand against the brick. "Do what?"

Except he knew exactly what Charlie was talking about. Because Charlie *always* cut right to the chase. His shyness meant he didn't talk much, especially when they were with the whole team. But Charlie was brilliant. Maybe even a savant. And when he spoke, it was always worth hearing. And *always* honest.

Charlie's fingers tugged at Jeremy's arm, and warmth seeped into his blood.

"Look at me," Charlie said, the unusual command of his words making Jeremy turn. "You helped save my life. You gave me and my sister a home. You've made a thousand sacrifices these past weeks." The wind blew longish dark blond strands across Charlie's intense blue eyes and he stepped closer, nearly backing Jeremy against the brick. They were evenly matched for height, which meant Charlie's eyes were right at Jeremy's. And so were his lips. "You are more kind and generous than anyone I've ever met. So don't pretend it doesn't hurt you that those guys died yesterday. And don't think I don't know you blame yourself for it."

A knot lodged in Jeremy's throat. Any other time, he would've cracked a joke about just how generous he could be. Complete with an eyebrow waggle. And an unspoken invitation. Now, he slumped against the brick and dropped his chin to his chest, his gaze blurrily focusing on the T-shirt Charlie had borrowed from him. It read, *That's too much bacon! (Said no one ever.)* His kidnapping made returning to his home for any belongings too dangerous to attempt, so Charlie had been digging through Jeremy's shirt collection to find the least innuendo-filled options.

Jeremy shuddered out a breath. *Of course* Charlie would know how he felt. Because the two of them were the only nonmilitary guys among the group, they'd often been thrown together. They helped the team behind the scenes by doing computer research with Marz or running communications and video surveillance when the team had an op out in the field.

When they weren't working, they'd fallen into the habit of hanging out together. Jeremy had volunteered to keep an eye on a very sick Charlie when he'd first been rescued, and they'd just sorta clicked. Because of Jeremy's habit of talking nonstop, Charlie had gotten to know him about as well as anyone did.

Charlie's injured hand slowly lifted, and Jeremy didn't miss that it was shaking just a little as it settled on Jeremy's hip. The contact stole Jeremy's breath, tight as it already was from the wave of emotion threatening to pull him under. His gaze whipped up to Charlie's. If it wasn't for the stubble roughening up the guy's square jaw and the wisdom in his eyes born of pain, his handsome face might've appeared almost boyish. But as attractive as Jeremy found him, he appreciated even more what a good friend Charlie had become, how he seemed to know what Jeremy was thinking without him even having to say.

"You should be inside celebrating," Jeremy said, his voice a raw scrape. "You and Marz did an amazing thing this morning." An hour ago, Marz and Charlie had cracked open a heavily encrypted microchip that contained a wealth of information that not only seemed likely to help the team clear its name, but proved that Charlie's father hadn't been dirty, like they'd all thought. "And I'm so happy for you about your dad."

A wounded darkness passed through Charlie's gaze, but he finally nodded. "Didn't feel right without you there." Pink filtered into his cheeks, and damn if that wasn't as cute as it was sexy. Jeremy wasn't sure anything had ever made him blush.

"I'm just not—" Jeremy shrugged and looked down at Charlie's chest again. Having seen the guy dress more than once, he knew that shirt covered lean muscle that ran from strong shoulders down to his narrow hips. Jeremy fisted his hands against the urge to burrow them under the hem of the tee. After weeks of looking, and wanting, he was *dying* to touch. Jeremy found Charlie hard to read though, and hadn't wanted to do anything to scare him off. "—very good company right now. I'm sorry if that—"

Charlie nudged Jeremy's chin up with his hand, his fingers just barely touching Jer's stubble-covered skin. And then his thumb landed softly against his lips.

Jeremy's heartbeat kicked up and his lips fell open. Slowly, oh so tentatively, Charlie stroked the soft pad of his thumb back and forth across them.

"Charlie," Jeremy whispered as arousal surged through his body, spiking his pulse, tensing his muscles, hardening his dick.

Uncertainty poured off Charlie as the man's hand

trembled where it touched him, but those blue eyes absolutely blazed desire. No way was Jeremy imagining that.

"You're always good company, to me," Charlie said in a low voice, his gaze dropping to Jeremy's mouth. Charlie leaned in closer, and closer still, and Jeremy could hardly believe the other man was the one to initiate this. But he was fucking thrilled.

Anticipating that first soft brush of skin on skin, Jeremy swallowed hard Charlie was so close his shaky breath caressed Jeremy's lips. His pace was maddening but so damn sexy Jer could barely breathe. And then Charlie's eyelids fluttered closed and he was right there—

Buzz, buzz.

Ring, ring.

Charlie jumped back, his cheeks bright red, as both their cell phones impatiently demanded attention. Frustration roared through Jeremy at the interruption, especially as he spied Nick's name on the caller ID.

Jeremy eyed Charlie as the other man checked his phone. Charlie ducked his head, averted his gaze, and hugged himself, and Jer hated the emotional distance that poured into the widening physical distance between them. Damnit.

Somehow, someway, Jeremy was getting that kiss.

Chapter 2

BREATHING HEAVILY, CHARLIE fished his phone from his front pocket with shaking hands. After working up the nerve to kiss Jeremy, he couldn't believe he'd chickened out when their phones went off at the same time. He'd been attracted to Jeremy from the very first time he'd awakened from a feverish sleep and found the guy sitting by his bedside. But it had taken Jeremy nearly falling to his death yesterday to finally convince him to act on that attraction.

The screen of his temporary phone read his sister's number. "Hey, Becca," he answered as he wandered to the other side of the ruined space.

"Hey. Where'd you go?" she asked, her voice bubbly and happier than he'd heard it since she'd engineered his rescue two weeks before. After everything she'd been through, she totally deserved happiness, and Charlie was glad she'd found Nick to share it with.

"Checking out the other half of the building with Jeremy." Just saying the guy's name heated Charlie's cheeks. Charlie wasn't a virgin, but he wasn't particularly socially skilled, either. Computers, he totally got. Games and puzzles, he could solve and decipher without a second thought. People? Half the time, he had no clue. So he wasn't sure if he'd read Jeremy's interest right or not.

Maybe Charlie wanted something that wasn't really there. Totally possible. After all, Jeremy was everything Charlie wasn't—outgoing, confident, funny. The sexiest man he'd ever known. Not to mention bisexual. So Jeremy could literally have *anyone* he wanted. Charlie was probably kidding himself thinking that might be him, a shy, awkward geek with a badly mangled hand and a whole bunch of bad guys after him.

What a catch.

"Well, listen," Becca said. "Nick doesn't want anyone out on the streets during daylight. At least not until Detective Vance gets the roadblocks set up around Hard Ink. Just in case . . ."

Right. Just in case . . . anything else happened. Like being kidnapped, caught up in an international drug-trafficking conspiracy, and attacked by mercenaries wasn't enough. Charlie couldn't believe this was his life right now.

"Yeah, okay. We'll head back," he said. That hammered the nail into the coffin of his botched attempt at a kiss. There were so many people currently living in the half of the building that hadn't been damaged that it was nearly impossible to have any privacy. Given how his father had disapproved of his homosexuality, Charlie had to assume the other former military guys might feel the same way. Nick seemed cool with Jeremy's bisexuality, but then again, Jer was blood. And Charlie certainly didn't want to do anything to endanger the only safe place to crash that he—and his sister—had.

So despite how much Jeremy's near fall had made Charlie want to act before it was too late, maybe it was better they'd been interrupted after all.

He hung up, then crouched down to retie the shoe-strings on his sneaker. The damn things wouldn't stay tight because his injury made anything that required two-handed dexterity nearly impossible.

"That was Nick," Jeremy said, walking closer.

Charlie remained focused on his shoestrings, like he had a chance in hell of getting them tied by himself. But it was better than facing Jeremy. "Yeah. It was Becca. For me, I mean. She said we should head back."

"Yeah," Jeremy said, crouching down right in front of Charlie.

Charlie stared at his beat-up blue-and-white Chucks like they were a long string of code that required his utter concentration.

"Charlie," Jeremy said, the request to look at him clear in his tone. But Charlie couldn't. He didn't want to see rejection in the other man's eyes, or have him make a joke about what almost happened. Between being kidnapped, tortured by a gang for information, and learning that his father wasn't what he thought he was, little felt real in Charlie's life right now. Not to mention the fact that the team had asked him to remain "missing," as far as the authorities and their enemies were concerned. They thought he'd be safer that way.

But the longing Charlie felt for Jeremy? That was real. It felt like the *only* thing that was real. And right now he wasn't strong enough to face the fact that it was almost certainly all one-sided.

Jeremy sighed and gently brushed his fingers away from the sneaker. "Let me help."

Humiliation heated Charlie's whole body. "It's just that these bandages—"

"Dude, I know. No worries at all." Jeremy made quick work of the laces. "Please look at me," he finally said.

Everything inside Charlie fought the request until it made him nauseous. Why couldn't he have been normal like Becca, or Scott, the brother they'd lost years before? Both of them had always been popular and outgoing and confident. They'd had tons of friends and dated and took charge of the world. Whereas everything had made Charlie anxious and jumpy, especially after their mom died when he was only twelve.

"Charlie—"

Meow.

Slowly, they both gazed toward the sound to find a big orange cat staring at them. A big orange cat with only one functioning eye. The eyelid appeared sunken and sealed shut where the other should've been.

Jeremy turned a big grin on Charlie. Despite his discomfort, that smile made Charlie's skin heat for a whole other reason. Between Jeremy's chiseled features, messy chocolate hair, full lips, pale green eyes, and multiple piercings, the guy made Charlie feel equal parts hot and unsettled—especially when he smiled, which he did *all* the time. At least until the attack yesterday.

"Dude," Jeremy whispered. "There's a one-eyed cat staring at us."

The corners of Charlie's mouth quirked up at the obviousness of the statement. "I noticed. Do you think he was in the building when it collapsed?" Dust and little bits of debris covered his fur.

Jeremy nodded. "Maybe. I've seen him around from time to time. But he's never come this close before. I didn't even know he only had one eye. Poor guy." Slowly, he extended a hand. "C'mere, kitty dude."

The cat tensed and his ears flattened. Jeremy stretched a little closer, and the cat bolted across the second floor.

"Damn," Jeremy said.

Charlie rose to his feet. "Probably spooked by the explosion."

Jeremy stood, nodding. "Yeah, he wouldn't be the only one. So, about that, thanks. Okay?" Those pale green eyes blazed sincerity.

Charlie frowned and wondered if Jeremy was seeming totally normal because he actually felt normal, or if he was pretending to act normal to ignore the hundred-pound almost-kiss in the room. "Uh, sure," Charlie finally said. Because he had no clue.

"Guess we better get back," Jeremy said. "Going down might be slipperier than climbing up, so let's take it slow."

Charlie nodded, and they started down the rubble

pile. About halfway to street level, the bricks slid out from under his feet, and Charlie almost went down. But Jeremy grabbed his good hand just in time and helped him the rest of the way.

Charlie tried to ignore how damn nice it felt to have someone hold his hand.

It was an unusual reaction for him. After his mother died, he withdrew in lots of ways, including from being touched. His father had never been touchy-feely, but their mother had smothered him with hugs and kisses. And then she'd left him.

Becca had tried to be something of a mother to him. She really had. But their mother's death made him feel like if *she'd* leave him, he couldn't trust anyone else not to do it, too. Computers were much more trustworthy that way.

When they reached the street, Charlie slipped his hand free. "Thanks," he mumbled.

"Sure," Jeremy said, raking his hands through his unruly dark hair as he turned back toward the building, his gaze scanning over the ruined façade one more time.

As bad as Charlie felt for Jeremy, he was glad to know someone understood just how profoundly his life had been turned upside down. Which was another reason Charlie shouldn't have attempted that kiss. He'd never made a friend as easily nor interacted as comfortably as he did with Jeremy. That kind of friendship was rare. No way should he do anything to jeopardize it.

"Okay," Jeremy said to himself. He turned back to Charlie, then did a double take.

The orange cat sat at the top of the brick pile.

Jeremy held out his hands as if the cat understood gestures. "Well, you coming with us, or what?"

The cat pawed at the top brick as if testing it for stability. But he stopped about halfway down and eyed them suspiciously.

"Maybe if we walk, he'll follow," Charlie said. Maybe the cat wanted to be close to them, but didn't know how to let himself trust them to actually get close. Gee, that sounded familiar.

"Yeah," Jeremy said, coming up beside Charlie. They walked around the rubble to the sidewalk that ran along the street side of the L-shaped warehouse. When they turned the corner along the undamaged side, Jeremy looked over his shoulder. "You're a genius. We're being stalked." He winked.

Charlie peered over his shoulder. Sure enough, the cat padded after them, occasionally pausing to assess his surroundings. At the other end of the building, they waved to a camera and waited for the electric fence to let them in and then turned left into the gravel driveway. A few moments later, the cat peeked around the corner.

Jeremy chuckled. One of Charlie's all-time favorite sounds. This man found joy in so much of life's littlest things, and Charlie couldn't help but admire that.

They turned the corner to the back entrance to Hard Ink, the tattoo shop Jeremy ran, and Jeremy punched in a key code that unlocked the door. "Come in, quick," Jeremy said, and then he bent and wedged a stop under the door that held it open a few inches. He gestured for Charlie to follow him up the metal-and-concrete steps.

Once again, the cat followed them in and to the bottom of the steps.

This time, Charlie grinned. "What do you think Eileen's gonna do?" Eileen was a three-legged German shepherd puppy that Becca had rescued off the streets. And the dog was *awesome.*

"Dunno," Jeremy said, mischievousness filling his green eyes. "But it should be fun to watch." He waggled his brows.

Two doors stood on the second-floor landing. They took the one to the cavernous warehouse space that had been a gym, but now served as the team's war room and everyone's dining room, too. Jeremy unlocked the door and propped it open.

They ducked behind a big shelving unit full of gym equipment. Moments later, the cat stuck his head in.

Beckett Murda came up beside them. "What's going on?" he asked in a deep, no-nonsense voice. The guy was linebacker big and always serious. If Beckett hadn't been involved in his rescue, Charlie would've been even more intimidated by him.

"Sshh," Jeremy said, so *not* intimidated that he didn't think twice about shushing the guy. "You'll see. Watch."

The cat came in, eyeballed them with its one big yellow eye, and bolted around them and behind another shelving unit.

"Seriously?" Beckett said.

Jeremy grinned and nodded. "Dude. It's a one-eyed cat. He fits right in."

The scars around Beckett's right eye became more

pronounced as his gaze narrowed, but the gym door pushed open again, cutting off whatever he'd been about to say.

"Hey. Why are the doors propped?" Kat asked, kicking the doorstop away. "The outside door downstairs was, too. I closed it." Jeremy's younger sister had arrived three days before and Charlie had nothing but respect for her, especially after she'd hightailed it up on top of the building yesterday to help defend them during the attack.

"Because we found a cat," Jeremy said excitedly. Charlie looked away for a moment, because he was sure they'd all be able to read just how frickin' cute he found Jeremy when he was all worked up about something. The guy radiated a positive energy that just made Charlie feel . . . alive.

Brow arched, Kat frowned at Beckett. "*You* found a cat, Trigger?" she asked, the nickname resulting from the fact that Beckett had apparently pulled his gun on Kat the first time they met.

Beckett glared, shook his head, and walked away.

Kat chuckled. "He's so easy."

"The cat was in the other half of the building," Jeremy said. "He only has one eye."

"From the explosion?" Kat asked. She was way shorter than Jeremy, but otherwise the family resemblance was clear. Chocolate brown hair, green eyes, an expertise in sarcasm.

"No. Looks like it's been that way a while. But he followed us home. Isn't that awesome?" Jeremy asked.

Kat laughed. "You always were the king of the stray

animals, Jeremy." She patted his arm, pushed onto her tiptoes, and kissed his cheek. "One of the many things I love about you. Hope Nick doesn't mind." She winked and walked away.

"Shit, don't tell him yet," Jeremy called.

She waved. "Good luck with that."

More people poured into the room, including Nick. The family resemblance between the brothers was clear, although Nick was about a million times more serious than Jer. Which, despite the fact that Nick had personally hauled Charlie's half-conscious body out of his prison two weeks before, made him pretty damn intimidating, too. Plus, Charlie couldn't help but wonder what the guy would think of his interest in his brother.

"There you are," Nick said to Jeremy. "I can't believe you skipped out on our celebratory breakfast. Becca even put chocolate chips in the pancakes."

Jeremy shrugged and the humor from moments before faded from his face. "Sorry."

"No worries," Nick said. "But we're meeting as soon as everyone's done eating. You in?"

"Yeah, of course," Jeremy said. Charlie nodded, knowing he'd be helping Marz set up additional computers so more people could work through the documents they'd discovered on the microchip.

"Then come on over," Nick said. "Because we've got work to do."

Chapter 3

JEREMY DESPERATELY WANTED a few more quiet moments with Charlie. He didn't think he'd imagined the guy's embarrassment after their phones had interrupted their almost kiss. Hell, Charlie hadn't even wanted to look at him. So Jeremy really needed to let him know the only thing he regretted was that it *hadn't* happened.

Because Jeremy's heart was still racing at how close he'd been to getting something he'd wanted for weeks. If he closed his eyes, he could almost feel Charlie's breath teasing his lips. And since he was standing right behind Charlie's seat at Marz's big makeshift desk, he actually could smell the cool, clean scent of the Ivory soap with which he'd showered.

But there wasn't a damn thing Jeremy could do right now. Not when they were surrounded by Nick's team, all their girlfriends, and a handful of the Ravens, too. The only person missing from their usual group was Ike

Young, who had worked as a tattooist for Jeremy the past couple of years and was also a Raven. Ike had facilitated the alliance between the motorcycle club and the team and was bringing the rest of the club to help them later this morning. That alliance had finally given Nick and his guys the manpower they needed to fight the Church Gang, who'd kidnapped Charlie, and a defense contractor named Seneka they'd only recently realized was somehow involved.

"Okay, let's get started," Nick said, standing in front of Marz's desk. His gaze ran over the group. "We've got a lot on our plates today." He counted off on his fingers. "First, Marz and Charlie are going to network more computers this morning so that more of us can read the documents we uncovered at the same time. I'd like all hands on deck for that we can get through as much as possible in the next few days and ascertain what we've got and how we can use it."

Nods all around. Everyone had volunteered to help. Jeremy was just glad to have something he could do that actually contributed.

"Second, we have a number of security measures getting put into place today. Detective Vance will be here shortly to set up roadblocks around the neighborhood. The official story is that a major gas-main break caused yesterday's explosion and the area needs to be cordoned off while authorities assess safety and undertake maintenance. He thinks that should buy us a few weeks of security, especially since this area is so sparsely populated and there aren't many people to protest the roadblocks."

Kyler Vance was a Baltimore police detective. He'd earned the team's trust after Nick's longtime friend, private investigator Miguel Olivero, vouched for the guy. Vance had proven his trustworthiness when he'd shown up to help during the attack. When Miguel had been gunned down as their enemies fled, Vance had vowed to help them however he could, starting with forming a cover story for the building's explosion and setting up a roadblocked perimeter that would, hopefully, keep them safe and allow them to stay put.

Nick sighed and frowned. A wave of grief knotted Jeremy's stomach. Miguel had been a good friend and something of a mentor to Nick since his discharge from the Army. But this situation allowed no time for grieving, did it? The thought had Jeremy turning to Emilie Garza, who sat in a folding chair behind Marz. Less than twenty-four hours earlier, she'd found her brother Manny's dead body in a gutter outside of Hard Ink. Her brother had worked for their enemy, Seneka, which was what led Marz to Emilie in the first place. But Manny had apparently become a liability, because Seneka had dumped him on the street during the attack. Jeremy wasn't sure he'd ever seen anything more gut-wrenching than Emilie's reaction.

"Third," Nick finally said, "Beckett is going to set up snipers' roosts in abandoned buildings across the street so we have a better chance of seeing what's coming at us." Nick turned to Jeremy. "You have more knowledge than anyone of the surroundings. Will you help Beckett?"

"Absolutely," Jeremy said, giving the other man a nod.

At this point, there really wasn't anything Nick could ask that Jeremy wouldn't give to keep his brother and their friends safe. Jer's tongue flicked at the twin piercings on his bottom lip as he began brainstorming locations. He'd explored a few of the abandoned buildings in the neighborhood over the years, and one place leaped to mind as a good possibility.

Gesturing toward Dare Kenyon, the president of the Raven Riders, Nick continued, "Dare will help with that, too, since his guys will be taking shifts with us. And he'll work up a security detail schedule using his men and ours."

Tall with long, dark hair, Dare always seemed serious and reserved. There was a stillness about him that revealed he was always watching, always observing, always assessing. And nice as he'd always been to Jeremy on the few occasions when they'd met, Dare gave off a dangerous, lethal vibe that commanded respect, if not a little fear. "The rest of the club will be here in a few hours," he said, his face set in a dark scowl. The Ravens were out for blood after two of their guys died yesterday. If they knew it was because of Jeremy . . . "So we'll be up and running later today."

Nick nodded. "Appreciate it—"

"We've got company," Marz said, stretching to look at one of the monitors. Jeremy's gaze followed to the screen, which showed Ike rolling in through the gate on his Harley. A helmet hid the identity of a passenger behind him. "Ike's here."

"Already?" Dare asked, frowning further as he exchanged glances with another Raven.

Moments later, Ike came through the gym door, his bald head making him identifiable even from a distance. Jessica Jakes, Jeremy's piercer and doer-of-whatever-needed-done down at Hard Ink, followed after him. What the hell was she doing here?

Ike's expression was so pissed it was almost glacial, whereas Jess, usually full of sass, was subdued. Almost . . . scared?

Jeremy came around the desk. In addition to being his employees the past couple of years, they'd also become good friends. And something was very definitely not okay. "What's going on?" Jeremy asked, looking from Ike to Jess. "Why are you here?" he asked Jess. He'd closed his shop to keep his employees and customers safe, so the last thing he expected was to see her back here.

She tucked her wavy black hair behind one ear, which highlighted one of the bright red streaks that ran through it, and looked to Ike.

"Someone broke into Jess's house last night," Ike said. "Ransacked the place."

Jesus. Would the madness never stop? "Are you okay?" Jeremy asked as Nick stepped beside him.

She blew out a breath and nodded. "I hid in a crawl space at the back of my bedroom closet until they left, and then I called Ike." Her brown eyes cut to Jeremy. "I knew you guys were shut in over here after what happened yesterday."

Nick nodded. "Did they take anything?"

Ike nailed Nick with a cold stare. "Only her computer."

"This makes no sense," Jeremy said, guilt flooding his gut for a whole new reason.

"Unless someone knows she works for you," Nick said. "And thought she might know something about me and the team."

"That's why I brought her here," Ike said. "They didn't steal enough to make it feel like a run-of-the-mill robbery, and the way they tossed the place seemed like they were looking for something."

Jess hugged herself, the position highlighting the colorful ink that ran up her arms—a lot of which Jeremy and Ike had done themselves. "But that's just it. I don't know anything. Hell, I didn't even know what all of you were doing here until Jeremy told me a few days ago."

Yeah, and that conversation hadn't gone great. He and Nick had lied to Jess initially, which Jeremy had hated. They'd thought she'd be safer if she remained in the dark regarding the team's investigation and enemies. In hindsight, Jeremy should've known better. Jess had made it crystal clear what she thought of their secrecy.

"Did you see the people who broke in? Did they say anything?" Nick asked.

"I didn't see anyone," Jess said, "but when they searched my closet, one of them said they needed me, whatever that means."

Becca came up beside Nick, and Jeremy was glad for the millionth time that they'd found each other in the midst of all this chaos. Because Becca was awesome and so damn good for his brother. "This feels like what happened to my and Charlie's places all over again. Someone looking for us and information they thought we had."

"I was thinking the same thing," Charlie said in a quiet voice from his seat at the desk.

"Shit," Nick bit out. "Yeah."

"Goddamnit," Ike said in a tone close to a growl. He scrubbed his hands over his bald head.

Jess's bottom lip quivered. "What now?"

Jeremy hadn't seen Jess this rattled in years, not since her dad had died within a few months of her starting at Hard Ink, and he couldn't hold back wanting to make her feel better for even one more second. He pulled her into his arms and petted his hand against her silky hair. She was so short that her head just touched the bottom of his chin. "For now, you stay here. I'll help you put your place back together when all this is over. Okay?"

A quick nod. "Thanks."

"Don't mention it, Jess." Her muscles trembled within Jeremy's embrace, and it was clear she was trying with all her might to hold back her emotion. But after having her house broken into and tossed in the middle of the night, who would blame her for falling apart? No one here, that was for sure. Jeremy looked toward Ike. "Thanks for being there for her, man."

His face still set in a deep scowl, the guy gave a single tight nod. Jeremy wasn't surprised at how angry Ike seemed. He'd always been protective of Jess.

"I'm sorry you got sucked into this mess," Nick said, bending down to peer in her eyes.

"Thanks," Jess whispered. And the civility of their exchange—when they usually drove each other crazy—proved just how serious this situation was.

Ike crossed to Dare, and they clasped hands. "When Jess called, I came into the city early. But the rest of the guys will be down by eleven."

Dare nodded, and looked to Beckett. "That'll give us time to set up those lookouts."

"Roger that," Beckett said.

"Hold up a minute," Nick said. "Before everyone scatters, I want Marz to show y'all something he's been working on. Marz?"

"I'm going to project some images on that wall," he said, pointing to the stretch of brick that ran along the side of his desk. Easy, his girlfriend Jenna, and Beckett moved out of the way. "These are stills I grabbed from the video surveillance footage during yesterday's attack." Marz was the team's computer expert, and the guy among all Nick's teammates that Jeremy had gotten to know the best. He was hilarious, dedicated to the point of pulling multiple all-nighters to get done the research they needed, and almost always upbeat.

Grainy images appeared on the wall next to a giant whiteboard filled with maps and questions and lists of information.

"Well, that wasn't too bright an idea, was it?" Marz said, chuckling to himself.

The brick obscured the images so that Jeremy couldn't really make out what they were. But it was more of the same all around, all the way up to the tall ceilings. "How about this?" Jeremy said, coming around to Marz. "Can I borrow your chair?"

"Sure, hoss. What do you have in mind?" Marz asked as he rose. The slight limp he had was the result of the prosthetic he wore. The ambush that had killed so many of the guys on Nick's SF team had claimed the lower half of Marz's right leg, too.

Jeremy climbed up on the chair, grabbed the small cube of the projector, and shined it down at the light-colored concrete floor right in the center of the group. Much clearer.

"Genius, Jeremy," Marz said, grinning.

"But, of course." Jeremy waggled his eyebrows and lifted the projector higher to enlarge the image. Everyone gathered around, those in the front taking a knee so people behind them could see.

"Okay, these first ones show that the license plates of the three Suburbans are all blacked out," Marz said, switching among images. Each one showed a version of the last—their attackers had smeared something dark over the plates. "So there are no leads there. Just an FYI." Marz glanced over his shoulder to Emilie. The pair exchanged some sort of silent communication and, finally, Emilie nodded and averted her gaze. "This image," Marz said, switching again, "shows the moment the attackers fired on one of their own." A flare of light was just visible on the far side of the middle Suburban.

"Manny," Nick said quietly, his tone full of regret. For Emilie. Even though her brother had been their enemy, they'd all gone out of their way to express their sympathies to her. Not only were she and Marz together now, but Emilie hadn't had any knowledge of Manny's criminal activities until Marz and the team told her.

Marz nodded. "Yeah. So it was clearly an execution." From what Jeremy understood, both the authorities and the Church Gang were hunting for Manny after he'd gone on a spree and killed a cop and several Church-Gang henchmen, so these guys had apparently decided he'd become a liability. Scary to imagine what they'd do to Nick and the team if this was what they did to one of their own. Marz switched images again. "Now, *this* is the best thing I found in reviewing all the footage."

The image showed a man firing from the rear passenger seat of one of the Suburbans, an automatic weapon in his hands.

"If you look at the guy's bicep, you'll see there's a mark," Marz said. "I spent at least an hour trying to enlarge and clarify it, and this is what I managed."

The new image that appeared featured a detail of that mark. Everyone leaned in. It appeared to be a silhouette of a man's head.

"I know it's not great, but when I pair the enlargement with this image—" A logo of a knight's helmeted head in profile appeared next to Marz's photograph. "—I think it becomes clear what we're looking at."

Murmurs rose up from among Nick's teammates.

"A tattoo of the company logo for," Nick said. "Sonofabitch."

"That's some of the best evidence we have, right there," Beckett said, leaning in to compare the images, "that Seneka was behind yesterday's attack. Which only makes sense if they were also involved in what happened to us in Afghanistan."

Running his dark hand over his close-cropped hair, Easy nodded. "Yeah. Because, otherwise, what would've motivated Seneka to attack?"

"Exactly," Marz said. "So now we've identified Manny as a Seneka operative and at least one of the other attackers, too."

"Finally we're moving past purely circumstantial evidence to the hard stuff we can use to nail them," Shane said, anger making his southern accent a little more prominent than usual.

Marz nodded and rubbed his hands together. "Now what we need to put all the details together is the information on the colonel's chip." Nods all around. "So Charlie and I will get to work on networking the machines and I'll set up an organizational system to keep track of which files have been read."

"Do it," Nick said. "For everyone else, if you don't have an immediate task this morning, rest up. Between reading those files and the watch rotation, there might not be much of that in the coming days."

The group broke up into side conversations, and Jeremy continued to hold the projector as a few people from the back came in for a closer look. When they were done, he finally returned the projector to the desk, dropped his hands to his sides, and shook them out. His shoulders had started to ache from holding the position for so long. Looking down, his gaze snagged on Charlie, who was giving Jeremy's body a good, long look.

Jeremy felt it like a physical caress as Charlie's blue eyes seemed to latch on to Jeremy's hips, groin, thighs.

Holy shit. So much desire radiated off the other man that it took everything Jeremy had not to climb down from the chair, pull Charlie into his arms, and kiss him until neither of them could breathe.

Charlie's gaze snapped upward and collided with Jeremy's. The blond man's face turned beet red and he made himself suddenly busy with some papers on the desk. Blood rushed southward through Jeremy's body, and he jumped down before his erection became obvious to everyone in the room.

There was only *one* person he would like to have made his erection obvious to. If he didn't find a way to get Charlie alone soon, he was going to lose it. He really was.

Jeremy scrubbed his hands over his face. When he dropped them, he found Jessica standing right next to him, her gaze glued to the computer monitor and her mouth hanging open.

He glanced from her to the screen, still filled with the image of the enlarged tattoo next to the Seneka logo, then frowned. "What's the matter?"

"Um, I don't . . ." She shook her head. "This can't be happening."

Icy dread snaked down Jeremy's spine. "What, Jess?"

Ike appeared on the far side of the desk. "What's going on?" he asked.

It was right then that Jeremy saw something he'd never seen before—Jess's cheeks filling with a bright pink heat. What the hell would make her blush, of all things?

"I, uh . . . I hooked up with a man who had a tattoo like that," she finally said.

"What?" Ike nearly roared. "When?"

Jeremy's stomach made a slow slide to the floor. *Please say it was a long time ago. Please say it was—*

"Friday night," she said, the words nearly a whisper.

Chapter 4

CHARLIE'S STOMACH KNOTTED as Jeremy groaned. In the time he and Jer had spent together, Charlie had heard a million stories about Jess—about how she and Jeremy had met, pranks she'd played or that he and Nick had played on her, and countless funny hookup stories. He talked about her enough that Charlie had at first assumed that Jeremy had something going with her, but when he'd asked, Jeremy had laughed and said he thought of her like a sister. Nothing more.

But that was a little hard to keep in mind when he hugged and held her like he had a few minutes before, and when he pulled her into his arms, like he was doing just now.

"Jesus, Jess," Jeremy rasped. "There's no fucking way this is all a coincidence."

"I didn't know," she said, her voice tight.

"Of course not. Don't you worry. Hey Nick?" Jeremy said, beckoning him with a wave.

Frowning, Nick cut through the group to them. "What's wrong?" Nick asked.

"This is so freaking embarrassing," Jess said, burying her face in Jeremy's neck. And hell if Charlie didn't feel like a little bit of an ass for the jealousy slithering into his gut. But, damn, what he wouldn't give to stand in the tight embrace of Jeremy's arms . . .

Nick, Ike, and Jeremy formed a circle around Jess, such that Charlie couldn't hear everything that was being said. But he heard enough to get the gist that a guy with a Seneka company tattoo had hit on her at a local bar on Friday night, they'd had a few drinks and talked, and then she'd brought him home. Which was how she'd seen his tattoo.

"So, you could identify this guy if you saw him again?" Nick asked.

"Of course," Jess said.

"Which was probably why they came looking for her last night," Ike said. "In the wake of the attack on Hard Ink, they were tying up loose ends."

A rock slid into Charlie's gut, and he felt even worse about his jealousy from moments before. Jess was in real trouble.

"Jesus." Nick tugged a hand through his hair. "Sure as fuck what it sounds like."

"I'm getting her out of here," Ike said after another moment.

"But she'll be safe here," Jeremy said. "With all of us."

Ike shook his head. "You've got enough noncombatants here as it is. And they're actively looking for Jess. I'm not taking any chances."

Charlie knew exactly what it felt like to be targeted, pursued, chased. After he'd hacked into the Singapore bank where his father had an account worth twelve million dollars and tried to learn who or what the depositor WCE was, he'd realized someone was searching for him in return. He'd packed up that night and went on the run. He'd spent the better part of a week moving from one hole-in-the-wall motel to the next until they finally caught up with him, stuffed him into the back of a van, and dumped him into hell.

"Shit," Nick said. "Maybe it's time we face this question once and for all."

"What question?" Jeremy asked.

Nick dug his hands through his hair and blew out a breath. "Whether or not to send all the civilians away until this is over."

"What?" Becca said, coming up behind Nick. "If I fall into the 'civilians' column, I don't want to go anywhere."

Her words drew attention, because the room quieted all of a sudden.

"What's going on?" Shane asked, his arm around Sara's shoulders. With the help of the whole team, Shane had rescued Sara and her sister Jenna from the clutches of the Church Gang a little over a week earlier, and now Shane and Sara were inseparable.

"We've got a situation and a decision to make," Nick

said as everyone gathered around Marz's desk again. "Looks like Seneka has been targeting Jess for a few days now and last night's break-in at her place was yet another kidnapping attempt. This situation is getting more and more dire. Ike wants to take Jess out of here 'til the dust settles. Which makes me wonder if we shouldn't send all the civilians away. Just 'til this is over."

Charlie's stomach tossed. Would they consider him a civilian? Or would he stay since Marz needed his help with the cyber side of their investigation? One thing was for sure, Charlie didn't want to go. He didn't want to leave the group that had saved him. And he sure as heck didn't want to leave Jeremy, the truest friend he'd had in a long time.

Silence stretched out for a long moment, and then everyone started talking at once.

"I'm not leaving as long as there's a chance any of you will need medical treatment," Becca said. She was an ER nurse and had been working with Shane, who had medic training from the Army, whenever any of them got hurt. Which was often. Hell, Shane and Easy both still wore bandages from gunshot wounds they'd received in a shootout with Emilie's brother at her house two days before.

"We may be civilians, Nick," Kat said, "but we can still help. You're going to need bodies to man the snipers' roosts, for one."

Sara pushed her long red waves behind her ears. "I don't want to leave. I thought the purpose of Detective Vance's roadblock was so that we could all stay here. Together."

Among both the men and women, a chorus of agreement rose up in support of staying.

"Okay, okay," Nick said. "I don't want to split us up either, but it was worth the discussion." He pulled Becca against him and kissed her forehead. Relief flooded through Charlie at Nick's words.

"Well, I don't mind going," Jess said, looking from Nick to Jeremy. "I'm sorry. But last night really freaked me out. I was so sure they were going to find me, and then . . ." She shook her head. "I can't even imagine what would've happened if they had."

"But where will you go?" Jeremy asked, taking her hand.

"To my place outside of town," Ike said. "No one besides the Ravens knows about it, so it's a good safe house."

Jess nodded. "You're sure you don't mind, Ike?"

His gaze narrowed and his jaw ticked. "Let's go. Now."

Jess turned to Jeremy. "Be careful," she whispered as she threw her arms around his neck. She did the same with Nick.

Ike crossed to Dare, but Charlie couldn't hear their exchange. And then Ike and Jess said their final goodbyes and took off.

"Jesus," Jeremy said, rubbing his forehead.

Charlie wished he was brave enough to go to the guy and offer him a hug, because he looked like he was starving for it. "I'm sorry," Charlie said, staring up at Jeremy's handsome face.

Jeremy gave him a nod. "Thanks. It just doesn't end, does it?"

Charlie rose to stand in front of Jeremy, and he had to ball his fists against the urge to rest them on Jeremy's chest or wind them around his neck. "It will. Don't give up."

Jeremy's pale green eyes met Charlie's for a long moment, and then he took a deep breath and nodded. "I won't. Thanks." Jeremy gave him a look that seemed like he wanted to say something more, but instead he just clapped him on the shoulder.

The heat of Jer's touch, casual as it was, lit a slow burn all through Charlie's body. After getting so close to kissing Jeremy, he couldn't seem to rein in his desire where the other man was concerned.

"All right, go chill out for a while," Nick said, pulling Charlie from his thoughts. "Marz and Charlie will let you know when they're ready for people to dive into the documents. And Beckett, Jeremy, and Dare will get the snipers' roosts set up." Nick raked a hand through his hair. His other arm remained around Becca.

For the first time, Charlie envied what they had—how easy it was, how natural, how open. As much of a hard-ass as Nick was, he never hesitated to show her affection in front of the other guys.

Charlie wanted that. He wanted that acceptance, that desire, that togetherness. Just once in his life.

The room finally cleared out except for Marz, Emilie, Nick, and Kat, who lingered on the other side of the desk.

"Hey, Charlie?" Kat said. "Do you have a minute?"

He had to resist the urge to look around and make sure she was really talking to him. He couldn't imagine what Kat wanted. "Uh, sure." Charlie rounded the desk, but she beckoned him to follow her toward the other side of the room where they were more alone.

"I just wanted to ask you if Jeremy is okay," she said, concern filling her eyes. They were a brighter green than her brothers', and heat crawled up Charlie's neck at the comparison.

"I think he is," Charlie managed.

"Is he blaming himself for the Ravens' deaths when the roof collapsed?" Charlie wasn't sure what his expression gave away, but then Kat frowned and said, "Shit. He is, isn't he?"

"Yeah. I tried to talk to him down, though. And I'll keep at it," Charlie said.

Kat squeezed his arm. "Please do. Thank you. You're good for him."

"What? Why would you . . ." He shook his head as the walls seemed to close in on them.

"Aw, I'm sorry. I didn't mean to embarrass you. I just thought . . ." She shrugged.

"What?" he asked, heat filling his face.

She looked at him a long moment, and then stepped closer. "If you two are interested in each other, I'd think that was pretty awesome. That's all."

Twin reactions coursed through Charlie. Excited surprise at her approval and acceptance, and bone-deep embarrassment that she'd noticed his interest. Had everyone? "Uh. Okay."

"You're too cute," she said. "No wonder he likes you." Why didn't the floor open up and swallow him already? Except, then he couldn't hear the answer to the question he was dying to ask. "Why would you say that?"

She smiled. "The way he gravitates to you. The way he looks at you, especially when you're not looking. And the fact that he's talked to you about what happened yesterday when he won't with me or Nick. And we've both tried."

"Oh." Charlie's brain struggled to process everything she'd said.

"I'll talk to you later," she said, when he didn't say anything further.

For a long moment, Charlie stood there, truly dumbfounded. Kat thought Jeremy liked him? And that Charlie was good for Jeremy? His stomach went for a loop-the-loop.

"Hey, Charlie?" Marz called from across the gym.

The words snapped him from his stupor, and Charlie crossed the space and hoped the others wouldn't realize how shell shocked he felt. "I'm here," he said.

"Good deal," Marz said. "Then help me kick some computer ass?"

Charlie smiled. Marz always had a way with words, and his easygoing, lighthearted nature put Charlie at ease. As did the fact that they both worked in the same field. It gave him a starting point of common interest with Marz that Charlie didn't find with many people.

And that was when Charlie realized that one of the worst situations of his life—being kidnapped and tortured—had led to one of the best. Before being grabbed by the Church Gang, most of Charlie's life had consisted of doing his computer security consulting services from his basement apartment. He'd been alone almost all of the time. Now, he had more friends and, frankly, just basic human interaction, than he'd ever had. And he didn't want to lose that.

"Yeah," Charlie said. "Kicking computer ass, it is."

"THIS WAS THE second location I had in mind," Jeremy said to Beckett as they entered the fourth floor of the abandoned warehouse diagonally across the intersection from Hard Ink. They'd already chosen the first location—the fifth floor of another abandoned building that stood a full block up the street and allowed panoramic views of Eastern Avenue, the main artery into Jeremy's neighborhood.

Beckett and Dare crossed to the windows, which had long since lost their glass panes. Beckett nodded. "Perfect vantage point of Hard Ink and of the approach from two directions."

Dare nodded. "You can even see the roadblocks," he said, pointing to something off in the distance.

Jeremy came up beside him and saw a truck unloading jersey barriers and fencing about three blocks down. Guess Detective Vance had come through. Glancing at Dare, Jeremy realized his gaze had latched on to something much closer. The avalanche of rubble still piled in front of the collapsed section of the Hard Ink building.

A rock formed in Jeremy's gut. From this vantage point, the whole building was visible from the roof down. His stomach tossed like he'd just crested the highest, sharpest hill on a roller coaster. Because he'd been standing on a part of the roof that no longer existed. And he'd nearly fallen three stories to his death.

Just as two other men had.

The words were out of Jeremy's mouth before he'd even thought to say them. "I'm so sorry your guys died, Dare. It's all my fault."

Nearly black eyes cut Jeremy's way. "How do you mean?"

From beyond Dare, Beckett's blue eyes stared at Jeremy, making it clear that Beckett waited for the answer, too.

"I froze. When it happened. If I'd reacted faster—hell, if I'd reacted *at all*, Nick could've gotten to them instead." The oddest lightness of being fell over Jeremy at the admission of his guilt to the man most likely to want to do something about it, even as his muscles braced for the consequences.

Dare's gaze narrowed, but then he shook his head. "Life deals us shit hands sometimes. Harvey and Creed got dealt theirs. That's not on you." He turned away from the window as if that settled it.

Jeremy released a long breath. Somehow, he felt simultaneously relieved and confused. Relieved that Dare didn't mete out some biker justice on his ass, but confused as hell about why his confession and Dare's apparent forgiveness didn't make him feel all that much better.

Beckett looked at him for a long moment, that piercing blue stare making Jeremy want to squirm. Finally, Beckett turned away. "Yeah. I think you nailed this one.

It doesn't even need the work the other location did." They'd had to haul debris away from the two windows they wanted to use in the other building, and shore up the ceiling over the window that gave them the best overlook of Hard Ink's street.

Just then, a distant roar rumbled from somewhere nearby.

"Sounds like the rest of the club's here," Dare said. "We good?"

Beckett nodded. "Jeremy and I can take care of provisioning the spaces."

"Good enough," Dare said, and then he disappeared into the stairwell. The sound of his boots echoed against the concrete and steel.

Scrubbing a hand through his short dark blond hair, Beckett turned to him. "Have you, uh, talked to anyone? About that?" he asked, gesturing toward the window.

Jeremy frowned and ducked his chin. Both Nick and Kat had come to his room to try to talk to him yesterday afternoon, but, really, what else were they going to tell their brother other than it wasn't his fault?

But who else did that leave to talk—

Charlie. And Charlie had been up there, so he knew what'd happened. He'd experienced it firsthand. He knew what it was.

Shaking his head, Jeremy stuffed his hands in his jeans pockets and said, "Not much."

Beckett sighed. "Look, I'm shit at . . . you know . . ." He waved as if searching for the word and hoping Jeremy would understand.

"Social interaction?" Jeremy offered with a wink.

Chuffing out a laugh, Beckett nodded. "Yeah, that. Fucking Rixey sarcasm. It never ends, does it?"

Jeremy grinned, not just because Beckett had unwittingly lightened the mood, but because he knew another Rixey who had been unloading all kinds of Rixey sarcasm on Beckett the past few days. His sister. "No, Trigger," he said, using Kat's nickname for the big guy. "It never does."

"Aw, for fuck's sake. Goddamned Trigger. It wasn't my fault that she—"

"I know. I know," Jeremy said, laughing. "You know, the more you let her get to you, the more she's gonna come after you, right? That's part of the fun."

Beckett scowled, the expression deepening the scars around his right eye. "Yeah, well . . . she doesn't get to me. So it's not a problem." He made for the stairwell. "Let's go."

"Uh-huh," Jeremy murmured to himself, still smiling. "If you say so."

"I do," Beckett said, starting down. "Can we be done with sharing time now?"

Jeremy kept his amusement to himself as he followed Beckett down, because it seemed to him that Kat had already gotten pretty far under his skin and the big guy just didn't know it.

Not that Jeremy could talk when it came to letting someone get under your skin. Because Charlie was definitely under his. The only difference was that Jeremy wanted Charlie there and absofreakinglutely planned to do something about it.

Chapter 5

AFTER HE AND Beckett loaded all the supplies into both snipers' roosts—sleeping bags, bottled water, snacks, ammunition, and binoculars—both regular and night-vision—Jeremy went back to the gym to see how else he could help. He found four new computers set up on a pair of folding tables and Becca, Sara, Jenna, and Kat already at work reading documents on them.

What he didn't find was Charlie.

"Need me for anything right now, Marz?" Jeremy asked.

The guy ran a hand through his brown hair and then he shook his head. "Nope. Looks like we have everything under control for these five minutes." Marz winked.

"Nick out with Vance?" he asked, wanting something to do. Some way to contribute.

"Yeah. The city sent a whole team of workers and it sounds like they're making good progress." Marz popped a pretzel in his mouth. "Lookouts all set up?"

Jeremy nodded. "Good to go."

"Show me where," Marz said, waving him around so he could see the computer screen. A map of the neighborhood appeared.

"What are those little icons?" Jeremy asked, looking at about a half dozen or more black circles that ran down the street.

"Our security cameras." He ate another pretzel then rubbed his hands together. "Okay. Where are they?"

Jeremy pointed out the two locations, and Marz marked them with an eyeball symbol. "Very apropos."

"Right?" Marz said with a laugh.

"So, uh, where's Charlie?" Jeremy asked.

"Hand was bothering him. As soon as we got the new computers up and running, Becca and I ganged up on him and made him go take a break," Marz said. "Guy's only two weeks out from an amputation. He needed some downtime."

"Oh. Damn. I hope he's okay," Jeremy said, concern crawling into his gut. He'd spent many hours at Charlie's bedside in the days after his rescue. The amputation site had been infected and Charlie had very quickly spiked a high fever that made them realize he needed further treatment. It had been serious, and not a little scary, for a few days there.

"He took some meds so I'm sure he will be. But I bet he'd enjoy some company," Marz said, grinning.

Was Jeremy imagining it, or was that smile just a little more suggestive than normal? Jeremy arched a brow at him, and Marz laughed. Shaking his head and chuckling,

Jeremy said, "It's a good thing I am supremely great company, then." He turned to go.

"Don't do anything I wouldn't do," Marz said, his tone dripping with innuendo.

Jeremy smirked over his shoulder. "Kinda leaves the playing field wide open, doesn't it?"

Marz laughed and nodded.

While it was always great to have a friend's support, Jeremy didn't actually care what anyone thought about who he saw. He'd put up with some punk-ass bullshit from people before when he'd gone out with men. It was sorta par for the course. You were going along, having a great time and minding your own business, when someone's bigotry just up and smacked you in the face. Like the time, back when he still worked for someone else's shop, when a customer refused to let Jeremy do his ink because he'd seen him out with another man. That shit didn't just sting, it fucked with his livelihood. Luckily, his employer and mentor, Aleck—the guy who'd made him see that his background in art could find an outlet in tattooing—didn't stand for that bullshit for one minute, and he'd asked the asshole to leave.

Not that Jeremy expected anything like that from these guys. Not when Nick had always been so cool with whoever Jeremy chose to be with. And not when the whole team had been so accepting of Charlie—hell, they'd risked their lives to save him—knowing he was gay and that Charlie and his father, who was also the team's commander, had had a falling out over it. Not one of them had blinked an eye. In fact, the only murmurings Jeremy had heard were ones of disappointment in the colonel.

Still, cart before horse much?

Yeah, probably. But there was one way to fix that, wasn't there?

Back in his apartment, Jeremy walked through the big open space that made up the combination kitchen and living room. With its exposed brick walls, unfinished industrial ceiling, and big leather couches, it was his favorite room in the whole place. Rehabbing an abandoned factory into a business and a kick-ass loft apartment—so far—was something he was hugely proud of. Whether it was drawing or painting or renovating or building something from scratch, Jeremy had always loved working with his hands, and buying this building had pressed every one of those buttons.

Usually, the big windows that stretched to the ceiling meant it was also full of light, but they'd hung blackout curtains to mask their presence in the building from outside eyes. Jeremy couldn't imagine—or, at least, didn't want to imagine—what might've happened during the attack if they hadn't taken the precaution of making it look like the other half of the building was inhabited and the inhabited half was abandoned and empty.

Passing the big kitchen island, Jeremy crossed into the hallway that led to all the bedrooms. His pulse kicked up at the thought of seeing Charlie, touching him, kissing him. Jer had nearly died yesterday, after all, so it was about damn time.

He paused in front of Charlie's bedroom door, took a deep breath, and knocked.

The door opened, the dim glow of a bedside lamp the only light in the room. "Hey," Charlie said. He dropped his gaze and stepped backward, as if he was inviting Jeremy in but uncomfortable doing it.

Jeremy wasn't having that. Not for one more second. Two steps had Charlie in his arms, their bodies crashing together, and Jeremy's mouth firmly, possessively, and unreservedly claiming Charlie's.

Burying his hands in the long strands of Charlie's soft hair, Jeremy devoured Charlie's lips and nearly groaned when he opened his mouth, allowing Jeremy to deepen the kiss. Charlie tasted like sweet, innocent temptation, and Jeremy wanted to consume every last bite. He stroked and sucked at Charlie's tongue, tightened his hands in his hair, and tugged their bodies flush until all Jeremy could feel, taste, and smell was Charlie.

Charlie moaned deep in his throat, and the sound shot right to Jeremy's dick, hardening him in an instant. Jeremy wasn't alone. The way they were pressed together made it crystal fucking clear that Charlie wanted this every bit as bad. When Charlie's hands settled on Jeremy's hips, then slowly, tentatively, so damn maddeningly stroked at his sides, his back, and then his ass, Jeremy groaned and finally had to break the kiss or risk having this be over before it'd really begun.

"Jesus, Charlie. I've been dying to do that for so long," Jeremy said, cupping the side of Charlie's face in his hand. Stubble tickled Jeremy's palm, and that roughness, that hardness, was one of the things he most loved about being with a man.

"You have?" Charlie rasped, his good hand fisting in Jer's shirt.

"Hell, yeah. I just wasn't sure where you were until this morning." Jeremy captured Charlie's bottom lip between his and sucked and tugged until Charlie's hips thrust against his. The motion rubbed their cocks together through their jeans, and the friction was both breath stealing and not nearly enough.

Jeremy nibbled and kissed at Charlie's jaw, his throat, the sensitive spot behind his ear. Charlie's hand grasped Jeremy's head, holding him and encouraging him not to stop.

"Aw, God," Charlie moaned. "Jeremy."

Damn, if Jeremy didn't love the sound of his name on Charlie's lips. He ran his tongue down the side of Charlie's throat until he reached the tendon that stretched to his shoulder.

"Can we . . . uh . . ."

Jeremy withdrew so he could look into Charlie's eyes. "What?"

Charlie's gaze darted toward the open door. He didn't even have to voice the words, because discomfort rolled off of him.

"Damn, I'm sorry. Wasn't thinking," Jeremy said as he pushed the door closed. "At least, not about that." He winked.

Heat rushed into Charlie's cheeks. "It's okay. It's just that . . ." He shrugged. "I . . ."

Wanting to put him at ease, Jeremy cupped his hand around Charlie's neck. "No need to explain, Charlie. I have no interest in sharing my first kiss with you with anyone else, either."

Charlie smiled, and it was such a rare thing to see. It totally lit Jeremy up inside.

"Are you okay with this? And are you feeling okay? Marz said your hand was hurting," Jeremy said, not wanting to take Charlie anywhere he wasn't ready to go, especially if he wasn't feeling good.

"I'm okay" Charlie said, dropping his gaze. "I don't want this to be over. I'm sorry I worried about the do—"

Jeremy kissed Charlie again, cutting off the words and hopefully allaying his concerns at the same time. Because Jeremy wasn't done. Not by a long shot. He pushed Charlie back one step, then another, until his back hit the wall. The most delicious moan spilled out of Charlie's mouth. Jeremy could've lived on those fucking noises if he had to.

The kiss went on and on. They nibbled, sucked, penetrated, and retreated until they were both breathless, hot, and so damn hard it nearly hurt. Their hands grasped and stroked and explored and their hips ground together as they pressed and thrust. The sounds of panting and breathy moans and shifting denim filled the room.

"What do you want, Charlie?" Jeremy whispered around the edge of their kiss.

"I . . . I'm not sure," he said, his blue eyes pleading. "Just . . . more."

Jeremy pressed his lips to Charlie's ear. "Can I touch you?"

Charlie nodded. "Yes."

"Anywhere?" Jeremy asked.

A shiver passed over Charlie's body. And damn if that wasn't sexy as hell. "Please," he whispered.

Slowly, Jeremy ran his hands down Charlie's chest, then his sides, until he could finally do what he'd yearned to do this morning—burrow under the T-shirt and touch him skin to skin.

Charlie sucked in a breath at the contact, and the sound both aroused and cautioned Jeremy not to go too fast. He had no idea what kind of experience Charlie might have under his belt, but nothing about him read as a casual sex kinda guy. Unlike Jeremy, for whom sex was unquestionably his favorite form of exercise. No better reason to get hot and sweaty.

He dragged his fingertips up Charlie's stomach to his chest, loving the feeling of his muscles jumping and twitching, until he exposed his nipples. Light blond hair thinly covered the center of the man's chest, and Jeremy licked his lips as a yearning to taste flooded through him.

"Take it off," Jeremy said. They worked the shirt off together.

"Yours, too," Charlie said, his words shaky and quiet. Like he was nervous. Or unsure.

Jeremy ditched his shirt in an instant, and his skin heated at how Charlie's gaze appeared to drink in all of the art covering Jer's body. "Look at me," Jeremy said. Blue eyes cut up to his. "How can I put you at ease? Because you don't ever have to be uncomfortable with me. You have something to say? I will listen. You want something? Ask. You need something? I will gladly give it. Every damn time."

"Okay," Charlie said, his tongue flicking over his bottom lip. "Then don't stop."

His grin was immediate. "I won't," Jeremy said, pressing a kiss to Charlie's lips, his neck, his collarbone. His tongue flicked at one hard nipple at the same time that his hands fell on the button to Charlie's jeans. Jeremy dragged the zipper down. Slowly. Together, they pushed his jeans and boxers over his hips.

"Oh, God." Charlie's head fell back against the wall as his erection sprang out into Jeremy's hand.

And holy. Fucking. Hell.

Charlie was hung.

He had a good ten inches of long, hard, hot cock.

It was like learning that unicorns were real.

"Jesus, Charlie," Jeremy rasped, standing back enough to look down between them. "Your dick is a thing of fucking beauty. Gonna take two hands to stroke you right." He gripped Charlie's cock tight in both hands and twisted his wrists as he stroked. Jeremy couldn't help but wonder what it would be like to have this monster inside him. Because while he'd savored the pleasure of another man's cock in his mouth, he'd never bottomed before. He'd never been serious enough about another man to give that part of himself away.

The groan that ripped from Charlie's throat as Jeremy worked his hands up and down his shaft was the sweetest thing. "Wait, wait, wait," Charlie said. "You're gonna make me come."

Jeremy grinned and gave Charlie a lingering kiss. "That was sorta the plan."

"But I . . ." Charlie swallowed hard and his hand tugged at the fly to Jeremy's jeans. ". . . want you to, too."

"Yeah?"

"Yeah," Charlie said. He managed to pull the button fly of Jeremy's jeans open with just the one hand, and then Jeremy pushed his jeans down over his hips. Charlie's gaze tracked his every move. "Oh, hell, you go commando. And you have a . . . a . . ." Wide eyes flipped up to Jeremy's.

Jeremy winked and took his dick in hand, stroking it as Charlie watched. He was shorter than Charlie but thicker, and two rings, one a blue circular barbell and the other a silver captive bead ring, hung from the tip of his cock. "A Prince Albert. Well, two of them."

"Didn't that hurt?" he asked, his gaze locked onto the movement of Jeremy's hand.

"Not too bad. And it made me so much more sensitive that it was worth it." Jeremy flicked his thumb over the piercings on an upstroke.

"Can I . . ." Charlie reached a hand toward him.

"Yes. Touch me," Jeremy said, pulling Charlie's fingers closer. A groan ripped up his throat at the first warm, firm grasp of Charlie's hand around his cock. "Fuck, yes." His own hand grasped Charlie's hard length again, and then they were jacking each other off as they alternated watching their hands move with breath-stealing kisses until Jeremy was sure the room spun around them.

Pre-cum coated their tips, and the way Charlie's

thumb swiped over Jeremy's head, catching the PAs every time, shoved Jeremy right to the edge.

"God, I'm not gonna last much longer," Jeremy said, his other hand cupping Charlie's balls.

"Me either," Charlie whimpered. "It's too good."

Jeremy sucked Charlie's tongue deep into his mouth, mimicking what he wanted to do to the man's cock. Next time. Because there would most definitely be a next time.

The moan that started low in Charlie's throat was desperately urgent, and Charlie pulled his mouth free from Jeremy's. "Oh God, coming. Coming."

"Looking at me when you shoot," Jeremy said, his heart absolutely racing. "Because I'm going to be right there with you."

"Aw, now, now. Jeremy." Charlie's eyes blazed with lust and pleasure and desire as the orgasm washed over him. He came against Jeremy's hand, his arm, his stomach.

Watching Charlie's ecstasy and feeling the warmth of his seed paint his skin was more than Jeremy could take. He came on a strangled yell, and watched as his cum marked Charlie's fair skin.

God, that was so fucking sexy.

A deep masculine satisfaction roared through him, and it made him want to mark and claim Charlie again and again. In any way. In *every* way. An odd thought for someone who'd never had more than casual encounters with men before.

Charlie collapsed against the wall, his chest heaving and his face more relaxed than Jeremy had seen in a long time. Maybe ever.

Jeremy smiled as he kissed Charlie's cheek, the side of his neck, his nipple. And then he bent over far enough that he could kiss the tip of Charlie's softening dick. He sucked the head into his mouth and flicked his tongue against it, and Charlie nearly buckled on top of him. Jeremy chuckled and rose, pinning the other man to the wall. He gave Charlie a long, deep, wet kiss. "Sorry. Just needed a taste. To tide me over."

"Tide you over?" Charlie asked in a breathy voice.

"Till next time," Jeremy said. "Because now that I've seen your cock, I'm not going to be able to live without feeling it in my throat."

A shudder ran through Charlie's body. "Jesus, Jeremy. So . . . you want . . ." He shrugged. "You want to be together again?"

"Dude." Jeremy leaned in for another kiss, then rested his forehead on Charlie's. "Yes. Again. And again. And again."

Chapter 6

A KNOCK SOUNDED from somewhere nearby. Not Charlie's bedroom door, but maybe Jeremy's, right next door?

Either way, the sound kicked Charlie's heart into a sprint for a whole new reason. Fear. Fear of getting caught. Maybe that was ridiculous, but when your own father disapproved of you to the point of cutting off all communications, that left a lasting mark. The team may have discovered that his father wasn't guilty of selling out his own men, but that did nothing to absolve the man for the way he'd treated his only surviving son.

"Someone's out there," Charlie whispered, tugging his jeans up and bending to grab his shirt. "Oh," he said, remembering he needed to clean off. He grabbed the towel off the back of the door and gave himself a hasty rubdown before passing it to Jeremy.

Jeremy chuckled as he accepted the towel. "I can guarantee no matter who it is, they've seen a penis before."

He buttoned his jeans, rehung the towel, and grabbed his own shirt.

Charlie hated to see all that beautiful ink disappear as the tee slipped over Jer's body, because what he really wanted to do was spend the rest of the afternoon exploring it and learning what every single piece meant to Jeremy.

"Still," Charlie said, wishing he could be like Jeremy and not give a damn what anyone else thought. Especially since what he'd prefer to be thinking about was how amazing it was being with Jeremy like that. How good Jeremy made him feel. How mind-blowing it was to be touched and kissed with such abandon. How hot it was seeing Jeremy come.

"Hey," Jeremy said, coming to stand right in front of Charlie.

Knock, knock. "Jeremy?" Nick's voice reached them from the hallway.

Nervous energy lanced through Charlie. After everything Nick had done for him and given how much he seemed to care for Becca, Charlie didn't want to do anything to damage his relationship with Nick. And Kat approving of them didn't necessarily mean Nick would, too. "Nick wants you," Charlie said.

Jeremy's hands gently clutched Charlie's neck. "Well, I want ten more seconds with you." He kissed Charlie softly, slowly, almost reverently. And Charlie wanted to just lose himself in it. He really did. Closing his eyes, he concentrated on the amazing contrast between the soft pull of Jeremy's lips and the cool bite of his lip piercing.

Which of course made him think of the piercing the guy had on his dick. What would it feel like—?

Knock, knock.

Charlie flinched. The knock was against his door this time. "Sorry," he whispered to Jeremy as he moved to open it.

"My brother has the worst timing," Jeremy muttered.

Charlie opened the door. "Hey Nick," he said, hoping his attempt to act like the guy's brother hadn't just given him a mind-blowingly good orgasm worked.

"Hey. Sorry to . . . oh, there you are," he said, looking over Charlie's shoulder to Jeremy.

"In the flesh," Jeremy said. He leaned against the door jamb, the picture of chilled-out ease. "What's up? Everything go okay with the roadblocks?"

"Yeah. Everything's fine. I think it's going to serve our purposes great," Nick said. "But that's not why I'm here. Actually, I'm glad I found you together. I have a favor to ask and it involves Charlie, too."

Charlie looked from one brother to the other, not having the first clue what Nick could want that would involve him.

"Name it," Jeremy said, his tongue flicking at the piercing on his lip.

Heat shot through Charlie's body at the sight. Damn. It had already been difficult acting unaffected by the guy when Charlie thought the attraction was all one-sided. Now that he *knew* Jeremy wanted him, it was all he could do not to jump the guy and make his promise of "again and again and again" come true right this very second.

The fact that he'd just come apparently bore no relevance to his dick, which stirred with interest and approval at Charlie's imagining.

Nick's voice pulled Charlie from his thoughts. "I was wrong about our commander. And I want to make it right, in every way I can." He tugged up the right sleeve of his plain white T-shirt. A tattoo ringed his biceps. The black silhouettes of six soldiers connected by the dark ground on which they walked. Nick's light green eyes fell on Charlie. "Given what I thought had happened, I excluded your father when I had this done. I want to rectify that. Right now."

"You want me to work on you?" Jeremy asked, pushing off the door jamb.

Nick nodded. "Please."

Charlie didn't know what to say. It was an amazingly personal gesture, and it meant a lot despite the fact that Charlie was so conflicted in his own feelings about his father. "That's . . . really good of you, Nick," he finally managed.

"It's long overdue," he said. Nick looked to Jeremy. "So, you game?"

"Absofreakinglutely." Jeremy followed his brother out of the room, then looked over his shoulder to Charlie. "Come with?"

Charlie was just about to protest when Nick turned and nodded. "Yeah, Charlie. You should come."

Surprise curled through Charlie's gut—both at being included and at how good being included felt. He spent so much time alone in front of a computer that he'd nearly forgotten how being with others chased the cold loneliness away and filled him with warmth. He hadn't had that in so long. A lot of which was his own fault. He definitely acknowledged that.

Down at Hard Ink, Jeremy led them through a darkened lounge space at the back of the shop and into a square room. He flicked on the lights, and the walls came to life with pictures of tattoos, large pencil drawings, framed memorabilia, and more.

"You can sit there, Charlie," Jeremy said with a smile. He pointed to a folding chair by the edge of a counter. Nick pulled another chair, this one with padded armrests and a back that appeared to recline, into the center of the room and sat.

Jeremy moved around with a calm efficiency born of experience. He looked the way Charlie felt when he sat in front of a computer, which made Charlie all the more fascinated with what he was doing. Charlie studied Jeremy as he made a stencil to add the seventh soldier into the current tattoo design and had Nick check its placement, as he cleaned and prepped his workspace, and as he poured black ink into a tiny cup and assembled the tattoo machine.

And then Jeremy sat on a rolling stool beside Nick and asked, "Ready?"

Nick gave a single nod. And then a low buzz filled the room as Jeremy dipped the machine's needle in the ink and leaned in to work.

Truth be told, Charlie was overwhelmed. Both by the significance of another man commemorating his father on his skin, and by how freaking sexy Jeremy was as he brought the image to life. Did Jeremy even realize that he kept flicking his tongue against the piercing on his lip? Because Charlie was about ready to combust at the sight of it.

The tattoo was done way too quickly. Charlie could've watched Jeremy work all day.

"Perfect," Nick said as he checked out the finished ink in the mirror. Jeremy bandaged his arm. "Game for doing one more?"

"It's like Christmas morning," Jeremy said. "When am I not game for one more? What do you have in mind?"

Nick pulled a piece of paper from his back pocket, unfolded it, and handed it to Jeremy. "I want it here," he said, pointing to his upper left forearm.

Jeremy's expression went soft for a moment, like whatever was on the paper moved him, but then he nodded. "All black?"

"Yeah," Nick said, sitting again.

They repeated the process with the stencil again, and that was when Charlie finally saw what it was. A tribal sun with an ornate letter *B* in the middle.

It only took Charlie a few seconds to understand Jeremy's expression. "Sunshine" was Nick's nickname for Becca. Nick was permanently marking his body for Charlie's sister.

"Does she know?" Charlie asked, gesturing to the stencil.

Nick shook his head. "Thought I'd surprise her."

"Might want a box of Kleenex handy when you do,"

Charlie said, glad that Becca had someone who loved her the way Nick did.

Jeremy laughed. "Right? I'm getting a little misty over here myself."

Nick cuffed him on the back of the head. "Shut up."

"Dude. Why do you always hit me?" Jeremy asked. "Seems a little imprudent when I'm about to get my hands on you, don't you think? I'm not above tattooing a Hello, Kitty on your grumpy ass."

That time, Nick was the one to laugh. "Do that and you'll wake up tomorrow morning with a shaved head."

Jeremy held up his hands. "That's not cool. You don't threaten a man's hair."

Charlie grinned as the exchange went on until Jeremy finally settled down and got to work. This tattoo took longer than the first, and had turned the skin on Nick's forearm bright red by the time Jeremy finished. But it looked phenomenal, the black stark and crisp on his arm.

Becca was going to flip out.

"Great work as always," Nick said as Jeremy bandaged the second piece.

"You're welcome, man," Jeremy said. Then, a moment later, he added, "You're that serious about her?"

Nick smirked. "You waited 'til after it was done to ask?"

Jeremy shrugged, a small smile playing around his lips.

"Yeah. I absolutely am. I'm that serious and I'm that sure." Nick smoothed a finger over the tape on his arm.

"Well, I'm glad for you. I really am. Becca's the best," Jeremy said.

"Way better than me. But somehow I got lucky." Nick

walked to the doorway and turned. "Can you two come up around seven and relieve the women from reading? They've been at it all day."

"Of course," Jeremy said.

Nick's words, though they'd been said jokingly, sat uncomfortably in Charlie's gut. "She's not better than you," Charlie blurted. Nick's pale green eyes cut his way. Rising, Charlie wondered why the hell he'd started this anyway. "What I mean is, you're every bit as good as she is. You saved my life, Nick. And hers. Hell, so many people around here owe you a debt of gratitude for what you've done. So, she's lucky, too. That's all I wanted to say." Charlie fisted his hands against the urge to fidget.

The silence seemed to stretch out forever, and then Nick held out his hand. "Thanks, Charlie. That means a lot."

Charlie returned the shake, although it was totally awkward given the bandages on his hand. They couldn't come off soon enough. And then Nick was gone.

When Charlie turned around, Jeremy was right there. "I really appreciate that you did that," Jeremy said, pulling Charlie into his arms. "Thank you. Nick's hard on himself, you know?"

Surrendering to the embrace, Charlie rested his head on Jeremy's shoulder and returned the hug. And it was such a sweet moment after how abruptly things had ended earlier. "You're welcome," Charlie said. "Is that a Rixey thing? Being hard on yourself?"

Jeremy gave a rueful laugh and pulled away enough to look Charlie in the eyes, though he kept one hand cupped around Charlie's neck. It made him feel claimed, wanted. "Maybe so."

"Because what happened on the roof wasn't your fault, Jeremy. And I hate that you're beating yourself up about it. I really do," Charlie rushed on.

"I'm working on it," Jeremy said, his thumb stroking back and forth against Charlie's neck. "I'm just so fucking sad about the way it went down." His voice cracked on the last word, and it nearly broke Charlie's heart.

Charlie pulled Jeremy into his arms, his hand holding and stroking the back of Jeremy's head. "Not your fault," Charlie whispered. Jeremy's hands fisted in Charlie's shirt and his muscles went tight, like he was holding back what his body wanted to release. Several moments passed, and Charlie just held Jeremy. It was easy to do. He'd wanted to do it for weeks. And he knew he could do it forever, if Jeremy let him. Because Jeremy made him feel present in the world in a way he hadn't . . . maybe ever.

Finally, Jeremy heaved a deep breath. "Thanks," he whispered against Charlie's throat. His breath was warm and ticklish.

"Any time," Charlie said, not wanting the hug to end. Not wanting the touching to end. An idea came to mind, and Charlie ran with it before he gave himself the chance to overthink it. "Would it make you feel better if I asked you to do a tattoo for me?"

Jeremy lifted his head wearing a grin and an arched eyebrow. "Seriously? Because it would be cruel for you to tease me," he said, his expression filling with humor.

"Aren't I pretty much always serious?" Charlie asked.

Which made Jeremy laugh. "Your sense of humor is wickedly dry, Charlie, but you definitely have one."

Charlie smiled and shoved his hands in his jeans pockets. "Good to know, I guess."

"So what would this tattoo be if you were to get one?" Jeremy asked, and then he leaned in for a kiss.

"Mmm," Charlie hummed as he let the kiss distract him. When the idea came to him, it was as perfect as if he'd spent months brainstorming and debating. Because there was one thing that had always held Charlie back in his life. One thing that kept him from having the things he most wanted. Fear. Maybe if he proclaimed his triumph over it, he could actually conquer it. A "fake it till you make it" kinda thing. "Got a piece of paper?"

Jeremy stepped back. "You're really serious about this?"

The more the idea gelled in his mind, the more serious he became. "Yes." Jeremy handed him a sheet of paper and a pencil, and Charlie turned to draw against the counter. He converted the letters to numbers in his mind, then wrote them down:

01001110 01101111 00100000 01000110 01100101 01100001 01110010

"There," Charlie said when he was done. "That's what I want."

Jeremy looked at the string of numbers. "Binary code?" Charlie nodded. "What does it mean?"

"No fear," Charlie said. "Will you do it?"

"Hell, yes," Jeremy said. "Where do you want it?"

"Somewhere private. Here, maybe?" he asked, gesturing to his side.

"Is this your first tat, Charlie?"

"Yeah." And no matter what happened between them, the fact that Jeremy was doing his first would always mean the world to him.

Jeremy frowned. "Ribs are likely to hurt more than some other places might. That okay?"

Charlie thought it over for a long moment, but his mind was made up. "Yes."

Before long, he lay shirtless on a padded table Jeremy had pulled into the center of the room and Jeremy was asking him if he was ready to start.

The first bite of the needle was easier to bear than he expected. Just as Charlie started to think getting a tattoo was no big deal, Jeremy would hit a place that hurt enough to steal his breath. And then he'd move on again.

"Doing okay?" Jeremy asked as he wiped at Charlie's side.

"Yeah," Charlie said, loving the idea that this sentiment was going to become a part of him. Then maybe he could actually live it. "Can I ask you a question?"

"Anything," Jeremy said.

Charlie breathed through a particularly intense area of the tattoo and then asked, "What is your *No Regret* tattoo for?" Jeremy had the letters inked on the back of each of his fingers. Of all Jeremy's ink, it was probably the one that most intrigued him, because Jeremy seemed like a guy who was totally satisfied with his life, a guy who had no regrets.

Jeremy continued to work as he spoke, his voice quiet and thoughtful. "Back when I first started working as a tattoo artist, a couple of things happened that made me really look at my life and think about who I was." He paused to dip the needle in more ink. "The first was that my father was not thrilled with my career choice. He'd always been supportive of my art, but he wanted me to doing something *real* with it, he said. Like be a graphic artist or go into advertising. We had a couple of rough years over that. Makes me wonder sometimes what he would think of the fact that I used the insurance money from my parents' accident to buy this place and open my own shop."

Charlie couldn't have been more surprised to learn that, like him, Jeremy had struggled to gain his father's approval. It made him feel even closer to Jer.

"The second," Jeremy said, continuing, "was that I had a customer refuse to let me do his ink when he remembered seeing me out with a guy at a club. It got pretty ugly, actually, and I was honestly scared that my boss would decide I was a liability and fire my ass. But then Aleck, my boss, ended up sticking up for me, and he became one of my closest friends."

"Are you still in touch with him?" Charlie asked, hating that someone as kind as Jeremy had been treated so badly.

"He died. Heart attack. It was part of what led me to open my own place," Jeremy said. "And then the last thing was that a girl I really liked couldn't handle the fact that I was bisexual and had been with men." A long pause. "All three of those happened kinda close together, and they shook the ground I was standing on for a while, you know?"

"Yeah," Charlie said. He could certainly understand how things like that would make you question yourself, even though it was hard to imagine Jeremy, of all people, experiencing a crisis of confidence. One of the things Charlie admired about Jeremy was just how self-assured and comfortable in his own skin he always seemed. What Charlie wouldn't give to be more like him.

"When I finally got right in my head with who and what I was, I got the tattoo. I wanted to remind myself to live life looking forward, not second-guessing every decision I've made and step I've taken." He paused again. "I'm not always successful," he said more quietly, "but I try."

Emotion nearly overwhelmed Charlie—admiration, respect, affection, and maybe even something more. Not that Charlie had much experience with anything more, but his gut told him he could very easily fall for Jeremy Rixey. Or, maybe, that he was already falling. "I really admire you, Jeremy," Charlie said.

"I really admire you, too, Charlie," he said.

Carefully, Charlie lifted his head and looked over his shoulder to where Jeremy sat. "Why?"

Jeremy paused and his light green eyes absolutely blazed at him. "Are you serious?" Charlie nodded, because he couldn't imagine what someone would find admirable about him. "Because you are a survivor. And you're courageous. And you're good in a crisis. And you're brilliant. For starters."

"Oh," Charlie said, laying his head down again. *That's how Jeremy saw him?* Because he sure as hell liked Jeremy's view of him more than his own. Maybe that was something else he could work on. Right after he conquered the fear thing. It didn't hurt to dream, did it?

"Can I tell you something else?" Jeremy said after a while.

"Of course."

"It's very unprofessional," Jeremy said, amusement in his tone.

"Okay," Charlie said, unable to hold back a smile.

"Putting my ink on your skin is making me really fucking hard."

Charlie's heart tripped into a sprint, the words heating his blood and engorging his dick. "Yeah?"

"Yeah." After another minute, Jeremy said, "All done." He wiped down his side and pointed to the mirror. "Take a look."

Charlie eased off the table and stepped up to the mirror. The line of black characters stretched down his whole right side. His skin was fairer than Nick's, so the black ink stood out even more starkly. Charlie loved it immediately. "It's great, Jeremy. Exactly what I had in mind."

The door clicked shut behind him, which did absolutely nothing to slow Charlie's racing pulse. Because the more he looked at the tattoo and thought about the fact that Jeremy had done it, the more just the idea of that turned Charlie on, too.

"I'm glad," Jeremy said, busying himself with cleaning up. He waved Charlie over. "Let me bandage you up."

Charlie stood in front of where Jeremy sat on the stool. He held his arm out of the way as Jeremy smeared on an ointment and loosely taped gauze pads to Charlie's side.

"All done . . ." Jeremy looked up Charlie's body. " . . . with the tattoo."

Chapter 7

THE AIR BETWEEN them sparked red hot, and Charlie was rock hard in an instant.

Jeremy noticed, his gaze dropping to the front of Charlie's jeans. Without any warning, Jeremy grabbed his dick through the denim and squeezed. "I want you in my mouth, Charlie. I want you hungry and needy and desperate to come down my throat. Can I have you?"

Charlie had never heard anyone say anything so hot in his entire life. With the room spinning around him, Charlie nodded.

Jeremy had Charlie's jeans open and down around his thighs within seconds. Jer grasped his dick and gave it a long, hard, wet lick from balls to head. A moan ripped out of Charlie. It had been a long time since he'd received head, and the fact that it was Jeremy doing it—sexy, funny, sweet Jeremy—was going to make it really difficult to make this last as long as Charlie wanted.

Another long lick up his length as Jeremy stared up at Charlie's face, those pale green eyes absolutely blazing at him, and then Jeremy took Charlie into his mouth.

Charlie's hands flew to Jeremy's hair.

Jer nodded and pulled off long enough to say, "You do whatever you want. Guide me. Hold my head. Fuck my mouth. Whatever you want, I want." And then he was on him again, sucking Charlie's cock deep.

At first, Jeremy sucked slowly as if exploring Charlie, getting a feel for his length. As long as he lived, he would never forget Jeremy's reaction to seeing him for the first time. Because, damn if it didn't make him feel good about himself to be so desired by someone like Jeremy. Charlie stroked Jer's hair as he settled into a slow, delicious, torturous rhythm, one that gave Charlie plenty of opportunity to feel the slick guide of the piercings on Jeremy's bottom lip.

God, it felt insane. Cold and hard next to warm and soft.

"So good, Jeremy," Charlie moaned.

And then Jer started moving fast, sucking harder, and taking him deeper. He ran his tongue all over the underside of Charlie's cock until he was panting and fisting his hands in Jeremy's hair.

When Jeremy impaled his throat on Charlie's length, the depth and tightness were so incredibly intense that Charlie shouted and grasped Jer's head, holding it tightly to him for a long moment.

Jeremy gasped for breath as he withdrew. "Yes," he moaned as he looked up at Charlie again.

Those eyes—and that look—would make up the stuff of Charlie's dreams for the rest of his life.

Alternating between fast and shallow and slow and deep, Jeremy sucked him better than anyone ever had in his whole life. And the intensity of the sensations, the piercing gazes from those green eyes, and the sheer knowledge of who was making him feel this combined to shove Charlie way too damn quickly to the edge.

"Oh, God, Jeremy. I'm gonna come. I'm gonna come." He hung on the edge for a long painful moment, and then he was falling, flying.

Looking up at him, Jeremy took him in deep and swallowed everything Charlie gave him. Jer stroked with his hand as he sucked, drawing the orgasm out until Charlie could barely stand.

When Charlie's body finally settled, they worked together to pull Charlie's jeans back up around his hips. Then Jeremy rose and kissed Charlie's cheek, his jaw, his lips. "Fucking loved doing that."

Charlie grasped Jeremy's face and kissed him deeply, tasting himself inside the other man's mouth, feeling the bite of his piercings, and hoping he could somehow find a way to communicate everything Jeremy was making him feel.

He could start by returning the pleasure Jeremy had given to him.

Sucking Jeremy's tongue deep into his mouth, Charlie grasped the button fly to the other man's jeans and tugged the buttons open. Jeremy gasped as Charlie gripped and stroked his cock. Remembering the way

Jeremy had groaned earlier in the day, Charlie swiped his thumb over the piercings on the head of his cock, loving being the cause of the pleasured sounds ripping out of Jeremy's throat.

He didn't ever want them to end.

"Wanna know a secret?" Charlie whispered around the edge of the kiss.

Jeremy raked his hands through Charlie's hair and his lips quirked up. "Sure."

Charlie broke the kiss but stayed close, his nose still touching Jeremy's. "I don't have a gag reflex." Just saying that out loud made Charlie's pulse race. He might've had a lot of insecurities, but there were some things about which Charlie was absolutely confident. Pleasuring another man with his mouth was one of those.

"Jesus," Jeremy rasped. "A ten-inch cock and no gag reflex. Are you sure you're not just a dream?" He winked.

Smiling, Charlie shook his head. "I've been thinking the same thing about you."

Jeremy cradled his face and his expression went serious. "I'm real, Charlie. *This*—what's happening between us—is real."

Charlie nodded as a warm pressure filled his chest. Did that mean he wasn't alone in feeling like this was more than just some stolen moments? And if it did mean that, if Jeremy was feeling more, too, would Charlie be brave enough to have everyone know the two of them were together? Just like Nick and Becca, or Marz and Emilie, or any of the other couples who'd gotten together since he'd been here?

He wanted to be brave. He wanted to live up to Jeremy's view of him.

No fear.

Right.

Charlie pressed a kiss to Jeremy's palm. Looking into his eyes, he said, "I want you to fuck my mouth. Just the thought of it is making me hard again."

Jeremy swallowed hard, as if the words physically impacted him. He flicked his tongue against his lip piercings and his eyes narrowed. "How do you want it?" Do you want to be on your knees at my feet or—"

"I can take you deepest if I lay down on the table and let my head hang off the end." It was possible Charlie's heart was going to beat out of his chest. He'd never talked like this—this explicitly, this directly, this honestly—with anyone before. But Jeremy's words from earlier still echoed in his ears, promising to listen, to give, to meet his needs. It made him feel safe to be vulnerable. To be real. To be himself.

"Get on the table, Charlie," Jeremy said, his voice like gravel. "Now."

Holding eye contact with Jeremy, Charlie walked backward until his legs bumped into the table, and then he got on and lay down. He pushed himself toward the end until his head hung freely over the edge, putting his mouth at the same height as Jeremy's hips.

Jeremy came closer, then leaned down to kiss Charlie. It was a little awkward since Charlie was essentially upside down, but he didn't mind because Jeremy's eyes and expression were absolutely blazing with lust and desire.

"Open your jeans and take your cock out," Jeremy said. "I want to see just how hot this makes you."

Charlie's hands moved to obey, arousal lancing through him at Jeremy's command.

"Fuck, you are hard, aren't you?" Jeremy stood in front of him and pushed his own jeans down to his knees.

The position gave Charlie a close-up view of the plentiful ink covering Jeremy's legs. His right thigh had a complicated geometric design all in black, whereas the left had a collision of tattoos that ran from thigh to calf—a compass rose, a wolf, a fierce-looking owl, and more, all tied together with tribal markings and punctuated by colorful flowers.

Jeremy dragged the tip of his thick cock over Charlie's lips, and Charlie opened as if he'd issued another command.

JEREMY COULDN'T BELIEVE that he was getting to experience this with Charlie, nor that Charlie had been the one to suggest it.

Gently, he pushed his cock into Charlie's waiting mouth and the sensation was fucking phenomenal. Hot. Wet. Tight. And having Charlie all spread out in front of him, his dick hard and jerking against his belly, just made it all that much more intense.

Rocking his hips, Jeremy penetrated and withdrew until his cock was slick from Charlie's mouth and begging him to move faster, harder, deeper.

And he'd thought having Charlie on his table before had made him hot.

He would never be able to look at this table again without remembering this moment. Without thinking of Charlie.

Charlie reached back, grasped Jeremy's hips, and forced him to go deeper. And the feeling of it was insane, especially when Charlie swallowed and Jer could feel the working of the man's muscles around the head of his cock. Charlie pulled him so close that he buried his nose against Jeremy's balls.

"Jesus, Charlie," Jeremy rasped. He braced his hands against the edge of the table. "That's fucking incredible."

When Charlie released his hold, Jeremy withdrew.

"What you said to me earlier," Charlie said, his hand going to his own cock, stroking and pulling. "Applies now, too. Do whatever you want to do, Jeremy."

Jeremy pushed into the other man's mouth again, and it was like something in his brain snapped. He couldn't hold back. He couldn't go slow. He couldn't be gentle. Not for one more moment.

Jeremy fucked Charlie's mouth, and the moans of approval spilling from Charlie's throat drove him on. Stroking Charlie's hair, his cheeks, his neck, Jeremy thrust and retreated until he was groaning and panting and wound so tight, he thought he might shatter. Not just because of the physical sensations. But because of *who* was making him feel this way.

Charlie.

When Jeremy told Charlie how much he'd admired

him, he meant it completely. Even before he'd known his father wasn't guilty of what they'd all suspected, Charlie had thrown himself into the team's investigation, helping however he could, denying himself sleep, and giving freely of his expertise. All that, despite the way his father had treated him. That took character. Integrity. Strength.

And then the way Charlie had spoken to Nick earlier, building his brother up and refusing to let the guy tear himself down. Charlie's words had gone straight to Jeremy's heart and reemphasized for maybe the hundredth time that Charlie felt like . . . family.

He'd never felt that with anyone else before. Man or woman.

The emotions fueled Jeremy's need to release, to let go, to claim.

Charlie grasped Jeremy's hand and held it against his throat, making him feel the movement of his cock deep inside.

"Fuck, Charlie. I don't want this to end."

But then Charlie started stroking himself faster, his fist tight and flying and twisting around the swollen head. The sounds he made became more urgent, more desperate, almost pained. And then a strangled moan ripped up Charlie's throat. He jerked his T-shirt up his chest and came in long stripes against his own belly.

It was too much.

Jeremy groaned Charlie's name, grasped his face in both hands, and held him tight as he buried himself deep and splintered into a thousand pieces. The orgasm was so intense, Jeremy saw stars and his vision went splotchy around the edges.

When it was over, Jeremy eased himself from Charlie's mouth and fixed his own clothing, then helped Charlie sit up until his legs hung off the edge of the table. Standing between Charlie's knees, Jer held the man's hands and gave him a million little kisses. For a long moment, they were just together quietly, their foreheads resting against each other.

Family.

Being with Charlie felt so damn natural. Like they'd always known each other. Like they belonged together. Like they were the best of friends—only so much more.

Family.

The realization that Jeremy was having these kinds of feelings about a man was surprising only because all his other encounters had been casual, just for fun.

But this was Charlie. And that made everything different. That made everything . . . . more.

Jeremy stroked his knuckles down Charlie's handsome face. "Thank you for that."

Charlie gave a small smile. "You, too. I've never . . . done that before with someone who was pierced."

"No? Was it different?" Jeremy asked.

His cheeks turned pink, just the littlest bit, and it made Jeremy smile. Charlie was adorable and cute and sexy as hell by turns. "It was like another sensation. Cool when your skin was hot. And harder against the back of my throat than I'm used to." Charlie peered up at him from behind longish lengths of his hair. "I really liked it," he said quietly.

Smiling, Jeremy pressed a kiss to Charlie's temple. "I really liked it, too." They both chuckled.

"I want you to know something," Jeremy said, taking a deep breath as he gathered his thoughts . . . and his courage. But he didn't want Charlie having any more doubts. Not about him anyway.

"Okay."

"I've loved the things we shared today, Charlie. For real. But what I'm feeling for you isn't just physical. It's something more. I'm not sure what yet, but I . . ." Jeremy shrugged. " . . . don't want you to think this is just about sex for me."

Charlie released a shaky breath. "It's not just about sex for me either. Even before today, I wasn't sure I'd ever had a friend as close as you. Now, to find a best friend and a lover in the same person. Honestly, I never even dared to dream that could happen for me."

Jeremy's chest filled with the warmest, sweetest feeling. He leaned in and kissed Charlie once, twice, three times—

"Hey, Jeremy," a voice said as the door opened. Kat.

What Jeremy noticed even more than Kat's interruption was Charlie scrambling out of his embrace and shifting off the table.

Not that his actions fooled Kat for one second. The knowing look in her eyes and the smirk on her face made that crystal clear.

Hurt pierced through the warmth that had filled Jeremy's chest a moment before, and he tried to push it back. Charlie was shy. A little anxious. And this was all still so new between them.

"What's up?" Jeremy said, squeezing the releases on the table so he could fold and put it away.

Kat looked back and forth between them for a long moment, like maybe she was debating giving them shit, but then she thumbed over her shoulder and said, "All hell's breaking loose upstairs. You might wanna come see."

Chapter 8

JEREMY FOLLOWED KAT and Charlie into the gym, won-
dering what in the world Kat could be talking about. They
weren't even all the way through the door before he knew.

Eileen had found the cat. Or vice versa. Either way,
the result was the same: pandemonium.

The puppy chased the cat in circles around, over, and
through the gym equipment, all the while barking and
yapping at the top of her little lungs. Every once in a
while, the cat would get cornered, and then there'd be a
series of hisses and a sharp yelp as Eileen pushed her luck
and got her nose swiped for it.

Jeremy couldn't hold back his laughter. "See, Charlie?
I told you it would be fun."

Nick marched across the gym to where they were
standing. "What in the ever-living fuck, Jeremy? A cat?"

"Aw, come on. He was over in the ruins. I couldn't
leave him out there," Jer said, chuckling as the cat finally

made his way onto a shelf of equipment Eileen couldn't reach. Didn't stop the runt from trying, though. "Besides, he only has one eye."

"Yeah, we noticed," Nick said. Eileen continued to bark up at the cat.

Shane, Marz, and Beckett joined their group.

"Can we keep him?" Marz said. "Because if we're going to have a three-legged dog and a one-legged man, then having a one-eyed cat is right up our alley."

Jeremy pointed to Marz as if he'd never heard anything more logical. "See? My thoughts exactly."

Nick's gaze narrowed. "Dude. The last thing we need is animal-induced chaos."

"Actually," Kat said, elbowing Nick. "Some animal-induced chaos might provide a nice distraction from the other kinds of chaos we're dealing with."

Nick rolled his eyes.

Shane rubbed his hands together. "That means we need a name." The other guys all groaned because Shane had been gloating for weeks that Becca had picked his suggestion of a name for the puppy.

"How about something pirate-y, like Matey or Patch?" Kat said.

"Those aren't bad," Jeremy said, grinning. "Come on, let's hear 'em."

"How about Willy?" Marz said. "You know, after Willy the one-eyed wonder worm."

The guys all busted into laughter. Even Charlie couldn't hold it back.

"That's so bad," Kat said, making them all laugh

harder. "What about Wink?" Nick said, getting more into the spirit.

"Or Blink," Shane said.

"Or Uno," Beckett said, trying to hold back a smile. Laughter and words of approval followed each new suggestion.

Finally, Eileen's barking died down, and Jeremy looked over to find her curled up at the bottom of the shelving unit directly below where the cat sat unhappily eyeballing her.

Becca joined them, followed a minute later by Sara and Emilie. "What are you guys up to?" Becca asked, wrapping her arms around Nick's stomach. He was wearing an old black Orioles long-sleeved shirt, which made Jeremy wonder if she'd seen his new ink yet.

"Naming this goddamn cat," Nick said, causing another round of chuckles.

"Oh, good. We're keeping him?" Becca asked.

"Of course, we're keeping him," Jeremy said, giving her a wink. "And thanks for being on my side, unlike your grumpy boyfriend."

"How about Minion?" Sara said. "Some of those little guys from that kids' movie only have one eye."

Jeremy crossed his arms and nodded. "Then I could say I have a minion. I like it."

"What about Peekaboo?" Emilie said, smiling. Jeremy really admired her ability to find humor so soon after experiencing such tragedy. Having come close to losing Nick in that ambush a year ago, Jeremy didn't think he'd be able to hold it together nearly as well as Emilie was doing if he lost his brother. "You could call him Boo."

"That's so cute," Becca said.

"Or Cyclops," Charlie said. "Cy for short."

Jeremy smiled at Charlie. "That's a good one. Cy. Cy the Cat. That's really good, Charlie."

Charlie stuffed his hands into his pockets and ducked his chin, but Jeremy could see the pleased grin he was trying to hide.

"Oh, God," Becca said. "We are really twisted people, with these names."

"How about Popeye?" Shane suggested, earning a new round of laughter. "Come on, that one's genius."

Just then, the door to the gym opened, and a bunch of Ravens poured in, Dare at the head of the group. Nick left their circle to touch base with him.

"Oh, I better go get dinner together. Everyone's going to be hungry," Becca said. "Excuse me."

"I'll help," Kat said to Becca, then she turned to the group. "It's potpie and last we checked, it smelled fantastic. We made six big pans, but I wouldn't delay grabbing a plate or there might not be any left."

"So, which name do you like best?" Shane asked Jeremy. "Popeye, right? It's totally Popeye."

Jeremy laughed. "I'm not sure yet, but we have a few winners here."

Talking and laughing, they all moved over to his apartment, and Kat was right—it did smell fantastic, like warm bread and savory spices. Becca and Kat scrambled to set out the trays of potpie and bowls of salad as a line formed at the island.

"How can I help?" Jeremy asked.

"Put all this over there?" Becca said, pointing to baskets of corn bread and containers of paper plates and plastic utensils piled by the sink. He moved them to the breakfast bar with the other food. It looked like they were feeding a small army. And, actually, he supposed that was about right.

All the Ravens and a few members of the team grabbed their food and took it over to the gym, where there was a big makeshift table that could accommodate a larger number. Jeremy and Charlie ended up on one of the couches in the living room, plates in their laps, along with Becca, Kat, Marz, and Emilie.

The conversation was easy and fun. Natural. Like they'd all known one another forever, not just for weeks. Once again, it had Jeremy thinking of family. And regretting the fact that, at some point, the investigation would end and everyone would go their separate ways. As big as the Hard Ink building was, Jeremy had never felt it was too big, even before Nick had been discharged from the Army and moved in with him. But now that he'd shared the space with all these people, he wasn't sure how he'd ever go back without feeling like he was rattling around in a tomb.

Was anyone else worried about what happened when all this ended? Stupid, really, since ending the investigation and nailing the team's enemies was the whole point. Not to mention that, as powerful as their enemies seemed to be, there was no telling when or even if it would ever end. And the longer it went on, the more danger they all were in.

Including Charlie. He'd already been kidnapped and tortured, and he'd been up on that roof yesterday morning, too. God, what Jeremy *should* be worried about was what happened if all this *didn't* end.

Jeremy turned his gaze on Charlie.

Amazing how, sometimes, really fucking good things came out of really fucking bad ones. The way Jer was feeling about the guy was so much more than good.

As casual as Jeremy had always been about sex and as few actual relationships as he'd had, finding and wanting Charlie was a revelation.

"What?" Charlie asked around a bite of corn bread.

Jeremy smiled and shook his head. "Nothing, man." As he finished the last of his potpie, he caught Kat smiling at him. This time, though, it wasn't a sarcastic or trouble-making smile. It was full of warmth and happiness. She nodded at him, her gaze skating for just a moment toward Charlie. And though he didn't need her approval, it still made him feel happy to have it. And lucky. Because both Kat and Nick had always supported him. No matter what.

After dinner, Jeremy and Charlie took a long turn reading documents. Marz, Emilie, Easy, and Jenna helped, while the others took up watch in the snipers' roosts or guarding the perimeter. Half of the Ravens took a guard rotation, while half slept, bunking down in sleeping bags on the gym floor.

By about one o'clock in the morning, the words on the screen in front of him started running together. "I'm afraid I'm starting to skim this," Jeremy said in a low voice. "And I don't want to miss something important."

Marz rubbed his eyes. "Yeah. You guys have been at this long enough. Call it a night."

"What about you?" Charlie said. "You've been here all day."

"I know, but—"

"Come up with me," Emilie said, cutting him off. A look passed between them and then Marz agreed and started shutting things down.

As they quietly crossed the gym, Easy fell in next to Emilie. "Thanks again for today."

"Any time. And I mean that, Easy." She smiled at him and then at Jenna, who gave her a hug.

"Thanks, Em," Jenna said, her dark red hair contrasting with Emilie's chocolate brown.

Emilie worked as a clinical psychologist, and Jeremy really hoped those words of thanks meant that Easy was getting help. Just last week Easy had admitted to the whole group that he was struggling with suicidal feelings. Jeremy didn't think he'd ever been in a quieter room than when Easy confessed what he was going through.

While the other two couples made their way up the steps to the third floor, where they were staying in an apartment Jeremy had only partially finished renovating, he and Charlie went back to his apartment.

Mr. Clean had apparently come through some time in the past few hours, because the wreckage of dinner had all been cleaned up. No doubt that was thanks to Becca and Sara, who'd been going out of their way to try to take care of everyone.

They crossed the quiet apartment and arrived at the door to Charlie's room first.

It had been way too long since Jeremy had touched Charlie, or held him, or kissed him. Pinning him to the door, Jeremy leaned in for a long, lingering kiss. Charlie tensed at first, but then melted into the kiss, his hands coming up to Jeremy's shoulders, his neck, his hair.

Jeremy wasn't sure what he wanted, but he knew what he *didn't* want.

He didn't want to be alone.

He didn't want to be apart from Charlie.

And he didn't want to play things safe.

"Come to my room with me," Jeremy said, nuzzling his lips against Charlie's ear. "I haven't had nearly enough of you yet."

Chapter 9

CHARLIE'S HEART RACED as Jeremy closed and locked his bedroom door. Which was a little ridiculous, given all the time they'd spent alone together over the past couple of weeks. But now, things felt different. Things *were* different. Because they'd admitted having feelings for each other, because they'd been together, because Charlie wanted to be with Jeremy in every way he could.

Which made him a little unsure. Normally, he'd just stretch out on Jeremy's bed, his back resting on pillows stacked against the wall. But he wasn't sure if that would mean something different to Jeremy now.

So he waited for Jeremy to take the lead. Standing in the center of the dark green room, one wall covered with more of the drawings he'd seen downstairs at Hard Ink, Charlie tugged his hands through his hair. It was just long enough that he could pull the top of it into a knot if he wanted, which he did sometimes when working at the computer.

"What's the matter?' Jeremy said, walking up to him. His hands settled on Charlie's hips, sending a zing of electricity through his blood.

"What do you mean? Nothing," he said, trying to sound relaxed.

Jeremy smiled. "Don't be nervous. We don't have to do anything. I just wanted to be with you. Nothing has to change between us, you know? I'm still just Jeremy. And you're still just Charlie."

That reassurance melted away most of Charlie's uncertainty and he released a deep breath. "Yeah. Overthinking it. I'm sorry."

Shaking his head, Jeremy cupped his hand around the back of Charlie's neck. Jer seemed to like to touch him that way, which was good, because Charlie absolutely loved the way it felt. Like Jeremy was claiming him, comforting him, and pulling him closer all at once. "Don't worry about that. Just talk to me, okay?"

"Okay."

"But you know," Jeremy said with a smirk, "if you find yourself feeling the urge to kiss me, that's good, too."

Charlie gave a small laugh, all of his tension draining away. "I might be feeling that urge right now."

Jeremy's thumb stroked over the side of Charlie's neck and his gaze narrowed. "Are you, now?"

Nodding, Charlie decided to put his tattoo into practice. He leaned in, flicked his tongue against Jeremy's lip piercings, and kissed him. Threading his hands into Jeremy's hair, he pushed his tongue deep into the other man's mouth, tasting, exploring, stroking.

Jeremy gave as good as he got, and soon they were breathing hard, and clutching tight, and grinding against one another until Charlie had to gasp for air.

"Lay down with me?" Jeremy whispered.

"Yes," Charlie said, letting Jeremy lead him to the big queen-sized bed. They stretched out on the soft flannel plaid comforter.

Jeremy pushed Charlie onto his back and climbed up over him. The other man's weight felt phenomenal as it pressed him into the soft bedding. "I like the look of you here. In my bed," Jeremy said.

"Yeah?" Heat filled Charlie's cheeks at the comment, but only because he loved it so much.

Jeremy nodded. "Me on top of you—is that hurting your side?" Charlie had taken the bandage off at Jer's instructions hours before, but the tattoo would take upwards of two weeks to heal, apparently.

"No," Charlie said, quickly sliding his hands up to Jeremy's back to encourage him to stay right where he was. Because Charlie would've endured just about anything to keep him there forever. "Kiss me, Jeremy."

"Gladly," Jeremy said, sucking Charlie's lower lip into his mouth. Slow, deep kisses quickly escalated to fast and frantic. Their bodies shifted and pressed. Their hands grasped and tugged. Their hard cocks rubbed together through their jeans until Charlie was suddenly sure of one thing.

"I don't want to come like this," he rasped, his brain scrambling to figure out exactly what he did want. And how to find the courage to voice it.

Jeremy pulled back, that pale green gaze absolutely on fire. "Then how?"

Charlie swallowed hard and his pulse raced even faster. Because his body, heart, and head were all in agreement, and he knew what he wanted—from Jeremy, *with* Jeremy.

Everything.

"I want . . ."

"Say it, Charlie. Tell me and I will give it to you." Jeremy kissed him with his eyes open, and it was so intimate, so close. Closer than he'd ever felt to another person.

"I want you in me," Charlie finally said, dizziness falling over him at the admission.

Jeremy kissed him, long and hard. "Are you sure?" he asked when they finally broke for a breath. "We don't have to rush—"

"I'm sure," Charlie said, clarity finally descending over him. "I feel so close to you. I want to feel that in every way."

"God, I want you," Jeremy rasped into a kiss. Charlie wasn't sure whether it was the kiss or the words that most stole his breath. All he knew was that he'd never felt so much, nor so intensely, as he felt right then. Affection. Desire. Love.

Love?

Could he really be in love?

Jeremy pushed up onto his knees, straddled Charlie's hips, and tugged his innuendo-filled T-shirt over his head. And Charlie was captivated by the sight of Jeremy over him. By the sexy way Jeremy shook out his dark hair. By the miles of ink that covered his muscular shoulders and lean stomach. By the friction caused from Jeremy's weight sitting deliciously on Charlie's lap.

Charlie's hands went to Jeremy's strong thighs as he stared up at him. "God, you're so damn hot." The grin Jeremy gave him had his chest ballooning with warmth and his cock aching.

Jer reached for Charlie's shirt and together they worked it off. Then Jeremy was on him, kissing his neck, his chest, his stomach. Deft fingertips found and teased his nipples until Charlie was panting and squirming and dying for more. When Jeremy's hands finally worked down the button and zipper to Charlie's jeans, he nearly cried out in relief. Slipping off the end of the bed, Jeremy tugged off the rest of Charlie's clothing and then removed his own.

Slowly, like a lion tracking prey, Jeremy crawled up the bed, pausing to kiss Charlie's ankle, to flick his tongue against the soft spot under his knee, to drag his teeth up the inside of his thigh, to nibble on his hip bone.

"You're killing me, Jeremy," Charlie rasped, nearly desperate.

His chuckle was as infuriating as it was sexy. "I think you can take it," he whispered, his mouth hovering right over Charlie's cock. He gave one long, slow lick up the length of it that had Charlie moaning and grasping at Jeremy's hair. Jeremy obliged him for just a moment, sucking his cock in deep and hollowing out his cheeks as he withdrew. And then he stretched out over Charlie's body again and kissed him so thoroughly, so passionately, so intensely that it made Charlie feel like he'd never been kissed before.

Charlie grasped Jeremy's head. "Want you now," he whispered.

Jeremy reached over to his nightstand and pulled open the drawer. He settled a condom and a bottle of lube on the bed beside them. "Turn over and get on your knees," he said.

Heart thundering against his breastbone, Charlie got on hands and knees. It had been a while since the last time he'd had sex, which was why he was absolutely starving for it right now. Despite how amazing their earlier activities had been, there was nothing like someone being wrapped tight around you while they were deep inside you.

Hands ran over his back, stroking down his spine and cupping his ass.

"You're so beautiful, Charlie," Jeremy said, pressing a kiss against the small of his back. "Don't let me do anything that hurts you, okay?"

"You won't," Charlie said, smiling over his shoulder. He adored the way Jeremy gave compliments so freely, so casually, like they were just plain facts. Charlie had never before experienced anything like it.

As Charlie watched, Jeremy grabbed the lube and coated two of his fingers. Anticipation made Charlie's stomach flip and then Jeremy was touching him with those slick fingertips, circling and teasing and stroking against the opening to his ass. One finger penetrated, making Charlie hum in pleasure. Jeremy caressed his back and ass cheeks as he fucked him with his finger, first one, then two. He twisted his wrist and scissored his fingers, preparing Charlie for more. For him.

The third finger made Charlie arch his back on a moan, but he was glad Jeremy was taking the time to make him ready. Jeremy's girth demanded it. And Charlie wanted to be able to take every thick inch of him. "God, that's good."

"Yeah?" Jeremy said, stroking his own cock, making the tip of it drag pre-cum against Charlie's thigh. "Your ass is fucking tight, Charlie. I'm gonna love it."

Gently, Jer withdrew his fingers and reached for the condom. He rolled it up his length and moved behind Charlie. The *click* of the lube lid sounded out, followed by the wet friction of Jeremy stroking himself again.

And then Jeremy was right there, nudging his opening, pushing in, and slowly—so slowly—sinking deep.

Charlie wasn't sure whose moan was louder. All he could think about was the white-hot burn of Jeremy's invasion. The way his cock filled him. The way it stretched him. The way it made him ache in the most torturously amazing way.

"Jesus, Charlie," Jeremy bit out. "Okay?"

"Yes, yes," he murmured, lowering to his elbows as Jeremy's hand pressed on his back.

The slow withdraw sent a flash fire of pain and pleasure through Charlie's body, and he reached beneath himself and grasped his own dick.

As Jeremy's cock penetrated deep again, a little faster this time, two things happened. The piercings moved inside Charlie, adding a whole new sensation to the already amazing feeling of being fucked. And the pain melted away in a heartbeat, leaving Charlie to drown in a sea of pleasure so sharp, so hot, so mind-blowing, that he had to press his face into the pillow to smother the groan that ripped out of him.

For a fleeting moment, his brain offered up the caution that Nick and Becca were right next door, but then Jeremy chased away his capacity for rational thought as he gripped Charlie's hips and thrust into him faster.

"You take me so good, Charlie," Jeremy said, his voice full of grit.

"That's because I need you," Charlie managed, a moan tearing up his throat as Jeremy bottomed out inside him. The piercings rattled together, almost creating a vibration every time Jer went deep, and it was fucking wild.

"I need you, too," Jeremy said. He sank deep and laid his chest against Charlie's back, his arms coming around Charlie's stomach. The position made Jer fuck him even deeper, and Charlie loved the sensation of being completely surrounded, completely covered, completely owned.

Jeremy's hips thrust and retreated while still hunched around him. It was so deep that a pleasure verging on pain flooded through Charlie, shoving him a giant step toward coming.

"Lay down, babe," Jeremy said, pressing a kiss against Charlie's neck.

Wait. Babe? Did Jeremy just call him babe?

Charlie's heart melted as he eased into a flat position on his stomach and Jeremy's weight followed him down, truly covering him from head to foot. It was one of Charlie's favorite positions because of the closeness, the heavy press of Jeremy's body, and the depth it allowed.

Jeremy grasped tight to Charlie's shoulder with one hand and gently turned Charlie's face to him with the other, allowing them hot, awkward, too-short kisses as they moved and writhed together.

"You feel so good," Charlie said.

The other man kissed him on a groan, his body moving faster, harder, deeper. As Jeremy picked up the pace, he forced Charlie's hips to grind into the bed again and again. The friction against his dick was amazing and tormenting and sure to get him there way before he was ready for this to be over.

Charlie moaned and reached back with one arm, grasping at Jeremy's ass. "Harder. Just like this. Gonna make me come."

"Fuck, yeah," Jeremy said as he delivered a series of hard, punctuating thrusts.

They were exactly what Charlie needed. The most exquisite clenching burn ripped through his lower body, and then he was smothering his yell in the pillow and coming in the tight space between his stomach and the bed, the sensation all the more intense because of the fullness Jeremy's cock provided.

"So fucking good, so fucking good," Jeremy rasped. "I can feel you. *God.*"

"Jeremy," Charlie rasped as the spasms finally slowed.

On a desperate groan, Jeremy pushed onto his knees until he straddled Charlie's thighs. He grasped Charlie's ass in both hands, his thumbs holding him open. Jer slowed his pace and made his strokes longer, pulling almost all the way out before plunging all the way in again.

"It's so damn hot watching me slide into you," Jeremy rasped.

Just imagining what it looked like made Charlie's dick stir again. "Feels even better," he managed.

"*Fuuuck,*" Jeremy said, falling forward again. He braced his weight on his arms. "I can't hold back any longer."

"Don't," Charlie said. "Come in me."

"Shit, Charlie." Jeremy's hips flew, the sound of their skin smacking together loud in the room. "Coming. Coming." Jer moved through the orgasm, a long moan spilling from his mouth, and Charlie felt the jerk of the other man's cock deep inside him.

Knowing that a man like Jeremy found such intense-sounding pleasure in *him* made Charlie feel like he was floating.

"Jesus," Jeremy whispered as his orgasm passed. He rested his forehead against Charlie's hair, then shifted the weight of his body to the side as he gently withdrew his cock. He got off the bed just long enough to dispose of the condom in the trash and to grab a folded towel from the dresser. "Roll over," he said as he climbed back into bed.

Charlie couldn't stop looking at Jeremy's face as the other man busied himself with cleaning Charlie's stomach and the bedding, because he wore an expression that was so relaxed, so satisfied that Charlie could barely believe he'd been the one to put it there. It made Jeremy beautiful, really, and it made Charlie's heart feel too big for his chest.

Finally, Jeremy stretched out beside Charlie and pulled him into his arms. Charlie's face came to rest on Jeremy's shoulder, the front of his body pressed fully against the side of Jer's. The moment was filled with the sweetest affection. Jeremy pulled Charlie's arm across his chest and then stroked lazily at his skin. He petted his fingers through Charlie's hair, making Charlie sleepy against his will. And he pressed kisses against Charlie's forehead over and over and over again.

"Stay here with me tonight?" Jeremy asked.

Twin reactions coursed through Charlie. Soul-deep satisfaction that Jeremy wanted him to stay. And anxiety about what would happen if someone saw them come out together in the morning. Could Charlie handle being outed already? Would anyone care? Would it cause the problems he feared it might?

No Fear.

The problem was, he was fearful. He didn't want to be. He hated it, in fact. But maybe he could fake it. The least he could do was try.

Charlie nodded and pressed a kiss to Jeremy's throat. "I'll stay." The words set off a fluttering sensation in Charlie's chest.

"Good," Jeremy said. "Because I don't want to let you go."

Chapter 10

CHARLIE COULDN'T SLEEP.

Every time Jeremy's warmth lured him into unconsciousness, he jolted back awake, his eyes going right to the alarm clock next to the bed, his brain caught in a frustrating state of alert caused by Charlie's worry about what would happen in the morning.

He didn't want to leave. He didn't want to miss even a single moment with Jeremy. He didn't want to give up this amazing closeness, something he'd never had before. So he stayed despite his exhaustion, despite his inability to relax, despite the adrenaline his stupid brain kept pumping through his system.

When the clock flipped over to 6:00 A.M., Charlie eased out of bed. He searched in the darkness for his clothes, able to tell the two pair of jeans strewn across the floor apart because Jeremy's had a cell phone in the pocket. Using the light from the cell to locate his shirt and shoes, he hastily put his clothes back on. He nearly held his breath in an effort to be quiet, and then he tip-toed barefoot across the room, slowly twisted the door-knob, and opened the door just enough to squeeze out.

Charlie nearly walked right into Nick and Becca.

"Shit," he hissed, so startled that he dropped his shoes and blood pounded behind his ears.

"Sorry," Becca said with a laugh.

Eyebrow arched, Nick gave him an appraising look.

Heat roared up Charlie's neck, and he bent to retrieve his sneakers. He was so, so busted.

"So, uh, you're up early," he whispered to the couple. His gaze skated to the door to Jeremy's room, still half-way open.

Nick's eyes narrowed, but a hint of a smile played around his mouth. "Did you . . . spend the night with Jeremy?"

Becca's eyes went wide and a slow smile climbed up her face.

The walls closed in on Charlie. His chest went tight and the air became suddenly too thin. Hastily, he leaned to grasp the doorknob and pulled the door closed. "Of course I didn't spend the night with Jeremy."

Crossing his arms, Nick smirked. "Then what were you doing?"

Charlie's thoughts whirled, his gut burning with guilt for lying to his sister and the man who'd saved his life. "I, uh, was going to get a clean shirt from him. I thought he'd be up," he finally managed.

"And you needed your shoes for that?" Nick asked.

Totally flustered now, Charlie shook his head. "I don't know. Why does it matter?"

Nick held up his hands as if surrendering. "It doesn't. No worries. I just thought maybe you two . . ." He shrugged. " . . . were together."

Oh God, oh God, oh God. Charlie felt totally cornered. Not only was he unsure how ready he was for others to know, he and Jeremy had never even talked about whether to go public in the first place. What if Jeremy didn't want anyone to know?

"No," Charlie blurted, his stomach burning. "We're not together."

"Oh. You're not?" Becca asked, her tone full of disappointment.

But Charlie couldn't think about that, couldn't analyze what it meant, not when he was struggling to breathe. "No. For the last time, we're not together. Gotta go shower," he said. He rushed down the hall to the bathroom and shut himself inside.

He didn't even turn on the light. All he could do was lean against the back of the door, his shoes still clutched to his chest. He wrote strings of code in his mind's eye until he could breathe again.

What the hell just happened?

You freaked out. That's *what the hell just happened. Idiot.*

Charlie heaved a deep breath, his lungs finally open enough to work again.

Wow. He hadn't had a panic attack that bad since the morning thugs from the Church Gang had busted into his motel room, forced a black cloth over his head, tied him up, and thrown him into the back of a van. Of course, it made a lot more sense in that situation than it did just now.

Flipping on the light, Charlie turned and rested his back against the door. Why couldn't he be normal?

"You know you're going to make things so much harder for yourself. Living like this," his father had said in their last argument about the long list of things he found disappointing about Charlie. It was an argument they'd had so many times. From the time Charlie had come out at nineteen to the very last. And at the top of dear old dad's list of WHY CHARLIE WAS A DISAPPOINTMENT AS A SON AND A HUMAN BEING was Charlie's sexual orientation.

"If things are harder, they're harder. But I'm not choosing this life, Colonel," Charlie said, knowing his use of his rank would irritate him. "It's who I am."

"You could try—"

"I'm gay!" Charlie threw his arms wide. "There's no trying anything. This is just who I am. I'm gay. I'm shy. I'm a loner. I'm a computer geek. I'm fucking awkward sometimes—"

"Language, Charlie. Show a little respect," his father said.

"Oh. Like you show me?"

"Respect is earned."

"And I can't earn yours as long as I'm gay, right? Fuck this," he'd said before he stormed out. His father had chased after him, but Charlie hadn't looked back.

Fuck this. Those were the last words he'd ever said to

his father. Less than a year later, Becca had shown up at his apartment and delivered the news that their father had died in Afghanistan.

Charlie threw his shoes to the bathroom floor and clutched at his hair.

The man was dead. And Charlie was twenty-six years old. Why the hell did his father still have so much power over him? Charlie wasn't sure whether to be more pissed at himself or his father's ghost.

All he knew was that, so far, he was doing a piss-poor job of living up to his tattoo.

His tattoo.

Jeremy.

Shit.

Even nervous as he was about everyone's reactions, Charlie felt like hell for denying Jeremy, for saying they weren't together. Guilt stewed in his gut until he was nauseous.

But he could make that right.

All he had to do was talk to Jeremy. Tell him why he was nervous. And see where Jer stood on the question of coming out to everyone else. For all Charlie knew, maybe Jeremy wanted to keep them quiet for now, too. After all, they were brand new and still figuring things out themselves.

Bending over the sink, Charlie splashed cold water on his face.

Just talk to Jeremy.

Charlie nodded to his reflection in the mirror.

That would make everything better.

Jeremy stood in the darkness and stared at the door for a long time after the conversation faded away. He'd awakened as Charlie attempted to slip out of his room, and gotten out of bed when he'd heard Nick giving the guy the third degree.

Which was how he'd overheard Charlie saying they weren't together. Twice. Three times, depending on how he looked at it.

After what they'd shared last night—hell, all of yesterday—Charlie wouldn't even acknowledge them to Nick and Becca? Both of whom obviously knew Charlie was gay and Jeremy was bisexual. Shit, as much time as he and Charlie spent together, Jeremy didn't think it'd strike anyone as a real surprise.

At first, Charlie's denial had set off an uncomfortable ache in the center of Jeremy's chest. Being denied like that sucked.

Charlie was shy, Jeremy was well aware. But it wasn't like the guy was still in the closet.

But then Jeremy had sat on the edge of the bed for a long time, head in his hands, replaying what he'd heard. And the more times he did so, the worse it felt. Not just like being denied, but like being rejected.

His heart hurt, like it was suddenly and violently empty. And then he realized why.

He was in love with Charlie.

He was in love with Charlie, and Charlie was denying to the closest people in their lives that they were even together.

Fuck.

And here Jeremy had thought *he'd* be the one to have problems coming to terms with choosing to commit to a man. After all, Jeremy was walking on totally new ground not just considering having a relationship with a man, but actually developing the feelings to commit to one. All the way.

And he had. Jeremy was all in.

All in love with Charlie.

Jeremy sat there so long spinning on what he'd heard and what it meant and what to do about it, that it was well after seven o'clock before he got his shit together, cleaned up, and made his way over to the gym.

Which meant he had no opportunity to have a private conversation with Charlie about any of it. And for now, that suited Jeremy just fine.

Because he was hurt, and that was making him pissed. It was probably better to chill his ass out for a while before trying to talk through everything with the man he loved.

When he entered the gym, the first thing he saw was Eileen, lying on her back, legs sticking up everywhere, as she stared at Cy, perched on a high shelf of equipment and glaring down at the puppy. Cy. Jeremy hadn't even realized he'd settled on a name for their newest resident until just then. Charlie's name. Of course.

Crossing the gym to the work area in the back corner of the room, Jeremy laid eyes on Charlie for the first time since last night. And just seeing him made Jeremy's body go haywire.

Red-hot desire spiked his pulse because being inside Charlie last night had been fucking amazing. Soul-deep yearning made his heart pang with want to touch Charlie again, to be with him, to claim him once and for all. And gut-punching hurt wracked through him all over again as his brain unhelpfully replayed the words Jeremy had overheard.

"Hey," Jeremy said as he approached Marz's desk. "Sorry I'm late. Overslept." Hard as it was, Jeremy didn't look at Charlie. Acting as casual as he could, he rounded the new table of computers and took a seat across from Becca and Nick.

"No worries, hoss," Marz said in his normal jovial way.

"I'll just dive back in where I left off last night," Jeremy said, busying himself with opening the files he needed and pretending to read his notes from the night before.

"Everything okay?" Nick asked.

"Yeah, sure," Jeremy said. When he realized Nick was staring at him, he finally looked up. "What?"

For a long moment, Jeremy was sure Nick was going to push the issue. Damn brother could be really annoyingly perceptive when you didn't want him to be. But Nick just shrugged. "Nothing."

Jeremy meant to look right back down again, but his gaze betrayed him, straying over toward Charlie.

Charlie was looking at him, and his whole face brightened when they made eye contact, his lips lifting into a small smile.

Well, that's fucking confusing.

Jeremy managed a single nod and ducked his chin, though he didn't miss the hurt flashing through Charlie's eyes at the lack of any normal greeting. But Jeremy didn't have it in him to put on a happy face this morning, not when it was possible that he'd fallen in love with a man who wasn't anywhere close to being there with him.

The whole morning went on like that. Jeremy would be sure Charlie was staring at him, and would look up only for Charlie to quickly look away. Or Jeremy would find himself staring at Charlie, only to pretend that he was absolutely engrossed in what he was reading on his monitor when Charlie noticed.

"Food break?" Marz asked.

Frowning, Jeremy looked at the little digital clock in the bottom corner of his computer screen to find that it was quarter after twelve.

"I'll throw some sandwiches together, if you like," Charlie offered. "I can bring everything back over here with some drinks. Or whatever."

"That would be awesome," Marz said.

Charlie rose and nailed Jeremy with a stare. "Wanna help?" He held up his bum hand.

Jeremy's heart tripped into sprint. The conversation he wanted to have with Charlie couldn't be compressed into the ten minutes it would take to make lunch. Assuming they'd even be alone over at the apartment. But he also didn't want to be put in the position of pretending nothing was wrong. "Sorry, but I'm almost done with a section of documents and I'd, uh, really like to finish it."

He felt like an ass making up the excuse, especially as the words seemed to deflate Charlie.

The guy hugged himself. "Oh, sure. Of course."

"I'm at a good stopping place," Becca said. "So I'll help." She got up, smiled at Charlie, and they left.

Jeremy tried to focus on reading, but found himself rereading the same lines over and over. By the time he got to the end of the briefing document he'd been working on, he had no idea what it said.

He sighed, and Nick and Marz both turned to him.

"What's going on?" Nick asked just as Marz said, "What's up with you and Charlie?"

Nick *and* Marz were gonna drill him about this?

Kill me now. "Nothing," Jeremy said, training his gaze at the screen. If he made eye contact with either of them, the jig was gonna be up.

A minute passed, maybe two. Jeremy glanced up to find Nick smirking at him.

"Dude," Nick said. "You're so full of shit right now."

"For real," Marz said. "Tension's been so thick in here all morning it's been hard to breathe."

Ooooor maybe the jig was already up. Jeremy groaned and hung his head backward. He ground the heels of his palms into his eyes. "Fuck."

"Does this have anything to do with Charlie walk-of-shaming it outta your room this morning at oh-dark-hundred?" Nick asked.

"Really? That's awesome," Marz said.

Jeremy glared at his brother and watched as Marz's smile fell.

"Wait. Why's that bad?" Marz asked.

"It's not," Jeremy finally said.

"So . . . are you guys together?" Nick asked, his tone

careful, like he knew where the mines lay in this conversation.

Heaving a deep breath, Jeremy shrugged. "*I thought we were.*"

The lightbulb went on behind Nick's eyes, and the sympathy Jeremy saw there felt like all kinds of shit. "Oh. Oh, hell. You overheard . . ."

Jeremy crossed his arms and nodded.

Across the gym, the door opened and a whole group of people streamed in. Charlie, Becca, Kat, and Beckett carried plates of food. Emilie, Shane, and Sara carried armfuls of bottled water and soda cans. Behind them were Easy, Jenna, Dare, and a few other Ravens.

"Come on over," Becca called. "Lunch is served."

Nick rose, came around to Jeremy's seat, and clapped him on the shoulder. "Just talk to him." And then he was gone.

"Ditto that," Marz said as he got up. "Hate seeing two of my favorite people so unhappy."

Jeremy nodded. He sat there for a few minutes debating what to do. Nick and Marz were right. They needed to talk. As soon as their shift was over, Jeremy would take Charlie to his room and hash this out once and for all.

Gonna be a long fucking day 'til then, though.

Yeah.

Jeremy got up to see Cy watching him from underneath Marz's desk. Crouching, Jeremy held out a hand. "Psst, psst. Come here, Cy."

The cat blinked once, twice, and then took a few cautious steps forward.

"It's okay," Jeremy said. "Come on."

Jeremy wasn't sure how long he sat there trying to coax the cat to trust him. Cy would take a few steps, then hesitate, then take a few more. But finally, miraculously, Cy was close enough to stretch and sniff his hand.

"See? It's okay."

Cy sniffed him again, then rubbed his head against Jeremy's whole palm, his one good eye closing like it felt so good, like he'd been dying for a pet but had been too scared to let anyone do it.

It had just taken time and patience and a little coaxing.

As Cy rubbed his body against Jeremy's legs, those words settled into his brain. What if those were all Charlie needed, too? Damnit, he really didn't want to wait until this evening to clear things up. The tension between them was eating him up inside, and Jeremy hated those flashes of hurt he'd seen on Charlie's face more than once.

Gently, Jeremy slipped his hands around Cy, testing to see if the cat would allow himself to be picked up. He did. And it made Jeremy grin.

"I got you, kitty dude. Don't you worry," Jeremy said, petting the cat's soft head. At some point, he'd need a bath and a trip to the vet to get checked out, but right now, all he seemed to need was some love.

Slowly, Jeremy rose, the cat tucked against his chest, and turned to find Charlie standing about fifteen feet away.

"You got him to let you pet him," Charlie said, not quite making eye contact.

"Yeah. His name is Cy, by the way." Jeremy walked closer to the other man, his gut clenching in regret at the invisible wall that seemed to stand between them.

"Yeah?" A smile flitted across Charlie's face, then disappeared again.

"Wanna see if he'll let you touch him, too?" Jeremy asked.

"Oh. I don't want to scare him," Charlie said, his voice so flat it was breaking Jeremy's heart.

Jeremy shrugged. "Don't worry about that. If you do, we'll just try again another time. I think he really wants some love, though."

Charlie slowly closed the distance between them. When he stood right in front of Jeremy, he held out his hand and let Cy sniff it, and then the cat let Charlie get as far as stroking his head a few times.

Raucous laughter erupted over at the table, and the cat exploded out of Jeremy's arms. Cy was no more than an orange flash as he bolted across the room and into a hiding place.

"See? He totally let you," Jeremy said.

Charlie lifted his gaze, and his eyes were such an amazing deep blue. "Jeremy?"

"Yeah?"

Emotions Jeremy couldn't read seemed to flit over Charlie's expression until he finally frowned and shook his head.

"What is it, Charlie?" Jeremy's gut tensed and his heart started to sink. Whatever Charlie was working up to say didn't seemed like it was going to be good. Sonofabitch.

"Just . . . damnit . . ." He tugged at his blond hair and dropped his gaze again.

"Char—"

"Fuck it," Charlie said. And then he stepped right up to Jeremy's body, grasped his face, and kissed him like Jeremy was the air he needed to breathe.

Chapter 11

IT WAS ENTIRELY possible that Charlie was going to have a heart attack. Because he was kissing Jeremy right out in the open, just like he'd always wished he could be brave enough to do.

And then the cheering and catcalling started from over at the table. No going back now, not that Charlie wanted to. Not at all.

But that didn't keep Charlie's pulse from racing so hard that he could feel it beating against his skin everywhere.

He just hadn't been able to take the distance between him and Jeremy for one more minute. And he couldn't stand being ruled by fear for even one more second of his life.

The instant his lips crashed into Jeremy's, Charlie realized something he'd never known before. Conquering fear didn't mean not being afraid, it meant being afraid of something and doing it anyway. It meant saying *no* to fear—no you can't rule me, no you can't hold me back, no you can't keep me from the things I want the most. Not anymore.

If there were going to be consequences for loving someone as incredible as Jeremy Rixey, Charlie would take every one. Because Jeremy was worth the risk.

When Jeremy moaned into the kiss and his arms threaded around Charlie's back, Charlie's heart grew so big inside his chest that it hurt in the most beautiful way. Ignoring their audience, he poured everything he had into the kiss until there was just them, this moment, this kiss.

Finally, they broke apart, their faces still touching.

"It's about frickin' time," Marz yelled to more laughter.

Jeremy chuckled and it made Charlie smile, even though his face was on fire and the room was spinning around him and the floor felt a bit wavy beneath his feet.

"Are you okay?" Jeremy asked, his hand slipping to cup Charlie's neck.

"I am now," Charlie said, taking a deep breath. "I'm sorry if you didn't want anyone to know about us, but I—"

Jeremy kissed him, cutting off his words, and then leaned his forehead against Charlie's. "I don't care who knows, Charlie. I don't care if everybody in the whole world knows. I only care about you."

Relief flooded through Charlie's veins. "Can we please talk?"

"Hell yes, we can talk." Jeremy took Charlie by the hand, their fingers intertwined, and led him toward the door. About halfway across the room, Jeremy waved off a new round of clapping and whistles.

Charlie stopped and looked across the room. They were all smiling at them. The whole team and all their girlfriends. Even the couple of Ravens he didn't know. Smiling and laughing, like they were happy for them. And it made Charlie happier than he'd ever been in his life—happy to have found someone like Jeremy, happy to have found all these crazy people, happy to have taken a chance.

"Hey Shane?" Charlie called. "The cat's name is Cy."

"What?" Shane said, shooting up from his chair. "That shit ain't fair!"

More laughter followed them out the door and into the quiet of the hallway.

"My room?" Jeremy asked, keying in the code to the apartment door with his free hand. His other hand still clutched Charlie's tight.

"Sure," Charlie said.

In Jeremy's room, they sat on the edge of the bed, thigh to thigh. Both of them started to talk at the same time.

"I did something stupid this morning—" Charlie began.

"Listen, I overheard what you said—" Jeremy said.

A long pause, and then Charlie said, "Oh, God. You heard me?" Guilt made his gut clench.

"Yeah," Jeremy said.

Charlie took Jer's hands. "I'm so sorry. I freaked out. We hadn't talked about whether to go public, so I didn't know . . ." He shook his head. "I froze. I let fear get the best of me and I lied about us. I'm so sorry."

To Charlie's surprise, Jeremy smiled. "I'd say you've beaten that fear now."

They chuckled, and Charlie shook his head. "Please say you forgive me."

"Of course I do," Jeremy said. "It's not even a question."

"I promise I'll never deny you again, Jeremy. I couldn't, because I . . . uh . . ." His heart tripped into a sprint, but he'd come this far, and now it was time to go all the way. To be totally honest. He owed Jeremy that after telling that horrible lie about not being together. And he owed himself, too.

"What?" Jeremy said, scooting close enough that he could stroke his knuckles down Charlie's face.

"Love you," Charlie whispered.

Jeremy's pale green eyes went wide. "What did you say?"

Oh, God. Too much? Too soon? Charlie dropped his gaze and shook his head, his thoughts all scrambled. "Uh."

"Look at me, Charlie. Please?" Jeremy said, nudging his chin with his fingers. When Charlie finally gave in, Jeremy's eyes were filled with so much softness and warmth. "You love me?"

Charlie managed a nod, because he didn't want to lie to this man. "Yeah."

"You surprise me over and over again," Jeremy said with a growing smile. "And I fucking adore it."

"You do?" Charlie asked, his throat tight.

"I do, because I love you, too, Charlie."

Charlie's whole body trembled at Jeremy's revelation, because they were words he never thought he'd hear directed at him.

"Aw, don't cry, babe," Jeremy said, swiping at the wetness he didn't even realize ran from the corner of one eye.

"I love when you call me that," Charlie said.

"Well, that's good," Jeremy said. "Because I like calling you that. Babe." He winked.

"Jeremy?" Charlie said, his thoughts whirling and his emotions overwhelmed.

"What?"

For a long moment, Charlie struggled to make sense of the mess in his head, and then the words spilled out, "I would've endured anything if it led me to you. I thank God that I'm alive, not because it freed me from those horrible men, but because it led me here. Right here."

"Fuck, Charlie," Jeremy said, his eyes going glassy. "And I would've given anything for you not to have endured it at all."

"I wouldn't change a thing that happened," Charlie said. "Because you are everything to me, and you were worth it all."

"I FEEL THE same way," Jeremy said, his heart more full than it'd ever been in his life. He kissed Charlie once, twice, encouraging him to recline on the bed. "However you got here, you're right where you're meant to be. At my side, in my arms, in my bed."

"Yes," Charlie whispered. "I love you so much." He wrapped his arms around Jeremy and pulled him in tight.

Jeremy's heart fucking soared, and he poured every bit of the euphoria he felt into his kiss. Their hands grasped and clutched, their lips tugged and pulled, their tongues circled and stroked until their cocks were hard and their hips were grinding together.

"I want you, Charlie," Jeremy rasped, pulling the other man into a sitting position so he could remove his shirt. Jeremy slid off the bed and toed off his shoes, and Charlie followed suit.

Clothing flew off between playful laughs and desperate kisses, their panting breaths and moans spilling into the room.

Jeremy hauled Charlie in close and grasped both their cocks in his hand, stroking the two of them while they kissed and sucked and groaned.

"I want your cock in my mouth," Jeremy said, nuzzling Charlie's jaw, "while mine's in yours."

Charlie nodded, took Jeremy's hand, and guided them back to the bed. And Jeremy absolutely loved it when Charlie took the initiative like that, because he knew it wasn't easy for the other man to do. His Charlie was so much braver than he gave himself credit for.

His Charlie. God, Jeremy fucking loved the sound of that.

Charlie laid down in the center of the bed and Jeremy climbed up over him, his knees on either side of Charlie's head. Jeremy took hold of Charlie's long cock just as Charlie swirled his tongue around the tip of his. They sucked each other deep, and Jeremy reveled in every moan that spilled from the other man's mouth.

Jeremy rocked his hips, fucking Charlie's mouth and feeling his throat muscles work around his cock. Charlie took it all, his hands massaging Jeremy's balls and squeezing his ass cheeks. Jeremy sucked on one of his own fingers, wetting it with his saliva, and then teased it against Charlie's opening until Charlie was lifting his hips and offering up the sexiest pleading moans.

When Jeremy finally penetrated him, Charlie sucked Jeremy's cock so hard and so deep that Jeremy had to fight back a scream.

One thing was crystal clear. Jeremy wasn't going to be able to spend much time in Charlie's mouth without finishing too soon.

"Fuck, fuck, fuck," Charlie rasped.

Jeremy pulled free and spun around. "I want you," he said, claiming Charlie's mouth for a kiss. Jer shifted to the edge of the bed and grabbed a condom and the lube from the nightstand, then turned to see Charlie flipping onto his stomach.

Which was when Jeremy realized that wasn't what he wanted.

"I've never bottomed," Jeremy said. He'd engaged in anal play before, of course, and he'd had one lover who had a big thing for toys, but he'd never been penetrated by another man's cock. Despite how adventurous Jeremy generally was, he'd never even considered it.

Charlie's blue-eyed gaze whipped toward where he sat on the edge of the bed, and the blond man smiled.

"I figured. And that works out great, because I've never topped. Unless you want to count one really awkward attempt with a girl when I was seventeen."

Jeremy stroked Charlie's back. His heart raced and his stomach flipped and he was possibly more turned on than he'd ever been in his life, even if he was a little scared—or maybe even because of it. "I was never serious enough about any of the men I saw to give them that part of me."

"I get it," Charlie said.

"I am now," Jeremy said, looking the other man right in the eye.

Charlie went still and his mouth dropped open. Slowly, he shifted into a sitting position. "Jeremy, you don't have to prove anything to me."

"No, that's not what this is about," Jeremy said, feeling the rightness of the idea down deep. "I'd just like for there to be one person who knows every part of me. And I want that person to be you."

"Oh, my God," Charlie said. "Are you sure?"

Jeremy smiled. "Absofreakinglutely."

"You realize I have no experience. And I'm probably going to last about thirty-six seconds," Charlie said, his cheeks going pink.

Jeremy chuckled and Charlie joined him. "I don't care about any of that," Jeremy finally said. "Will you?"

"Yes," Charlie whispered. "Uh, what position do you want to . . . ?"

Climbing up onto the bed, Jeremy handed the lube and condom to Charlie and got onto his hands and knees.

Charlie moved behind Jeremy, making Jer's heart take fast flight.

The click of the lube cap. And then Charlie circled two fingers against Jeremy's asshole while he rubbed his slickened thumb against the skin between his opening and his balls.

Jeremy moaned as Charlie slowly inserted a finger while still applying pressure against his taint. Charlie's other hand stroked his back, his ass, his thigh, relaxing Jeremy as Charlie prepared him. Although, shit, there wasn't any finger that was going to prepare him for Charlie's ten inches. For real.

Charlie chased the thoughts away when he added another slick finger and then rubbed them against a place inside Jeremy that made him gasp.

"Too much?" Charlie asked, his fingers stroking over his prostate again and again.

"Shit, no," Jeremy rasped. "It's just really intense."

Charlie chuckled. And damn if that wasn't fucking sexy.

After a few minutes, Charlie added a third finger. The stretching stung, but then Charlie reached underneath Jeremy and grabbed his cock. The stroking eased the burn, or maybe it was just that his body got used to it, but either way, Jeremy felt hotter and needier than he'd ever felt in his life.

"Now, Charlie," he said. Charlie eased his fingers free, and Jeremy groaned. "Lots of lube, please. Like, the whole bottle maybe." He looked over his shoulder at the other man and winked.

Charlie smiled from underneath long strands of hair and bit down on his lip. "Don't worry, Jeremy. I'll take care of you right." He rolled on the condom and slicked up his long length. "Ready?"

"Want you, Charlie. Yes." When he felt the head of Charlie's cock right there, Jeremy took a deep breath and bore down, knowing that would help open himself to Charlie's invasion. The first inch or two burned, but Charlie went slow, sinking deeper and deeper until Jeremy groaned at the crazy hot sensation of fullness. Finally, Charlie paused, holding himself deep inside as he reached around to stroke Jeremy's cock. The combination of the pleasure with the pain was heady and overwhelming, and pleasure gained ground as Charlie started to move in a series of shallow thrusts and retreats.

"Damnit, Jeremy. You're so tight that thirty-six seconds might've been optimistic," Charlie said in a strained voice.

A single laugh burst out of Jeremy. "Think of something that's not sexy."

"You are totally overestimating my capacity for thought right now. Shit," he said, his hips rocking against Jeremy's ass.

Jeremy looked over his shoulder. "Whatever happens, it's already perfect, babe." And Jeremy meant that, because the intimacy of their actions meant so much to Jeremy that he could never regret it. Not for an instant.

Charlie gripped Jeremy's hip with one hand and caressed his back with the other as he settled into a slow, deep grind. The vulnerability of the act, the stretching fullness it made Jer feel, and the incredible sounds spilling from Charlie's throat all combined to make Jeremy hard and hot and achy.

"I want to touch more of you," Charlie rasped. "Lay on your side?"

They pulled apart as they changed positions and then Charlie's stomach was tight against Jeremy's back. Charlie added more lube and then pushed in again.

Jeremy breathed through the initial burn until Charlie settled into a rhythm that had Jeremy panting and moaning and stroking himself in time with Charlie's hips.

"Let me," Charlie whispered, brushing his hand away. He kissed Jeremy's shoulder, his back, his arm as he fisted Jeremy's cock and fucked him so goddamn good. "Love you, Jeremy."

It was the words that did it. Jeremy was suddenly right on the edge and falling fast. "Fuck, gonna come."

"Yeah?" Charlie's hand tightened and moved faster around his cock.

And then Jeremy's orgasm nailed him in the back, stole his breath, and roared through him. And it was like he'd never come before, because being filled so completely added a whole other level of intensity to his release. Charlie stroked him through it and he came so long and so hard that he got light-headed.

Charlie moaned, his hips moving harder, faster. "Love you, love you," he rasped, and then his cock was jerking inside Jeremy. That sensation was so unexpectedly sexy that Jeremy found himself pressing back onto Charlie's dick, taking him even deeper, giving him every ounce of pleasure he could.

Charlie heaved a long breath against Jeremy's back and wrapped both arms around his chest. He squeezed Jeremy so tight that it was hard to breathe, but Jeremy wouldn't have traded it for anything. This closeness. This intimacy. This absolute fucking perfection.

After a long moment, Charlie withdrew from Jer's body. He got off the bed to dispose of the condom, and Jeremy hated every second of separation from the man who owned his heart.

Charlie climbed back into bed and snuggled in tight, his stomach to Jer's back again. "How was it?" Charlie whispered.

Needing to see Charlie's beautiful eyes, Jeremy turned in the tight embrace of his arms. Their faces were close, their breaths mingled, and their legs intertwined.

"It was amazing. Perfect," Jeremy said, stealing a soft kiss. "I just may not be able to sit for a day or two." He winked.

Charlie grinned. "Well," he said, peering at Jeremy through strands of blond hair that had fallen across his face. "Every time you feel a twinge just remember it was because I was inside you."

"Damn, Charlie. That was sexy as fuck," Jeremy said, kissing him deeply and totally loving the idea of the reminder.

For a while, they lay quietly, just staring into each other's eyes, not talking or kissing, just touching and looking and being present in the moment.

How could this day get any better?

Suddenly, Jeremy knew exactly what would make it

better. "There's one more thing I want," he said in a quiet voice, his heart beating a little faster.

"What's that?" Charlie asked, lazily stroking his fingers against Jeremy's back.

"Move in here with me," Jeremy said, the rightness of the idea settling deep inside his chest. Just thinking of Charlie's belongings mixed up with his and waking up with Charlie in his arms every morning was enough to make his dick stir again. "We don't have to do it right away if you need time to adjust to us, but—"

"Really?" Charlie asked, something close to awe filling his expression. "You really . . . want me . . . to . . ."

"Charlie Merritt," Jeremy said, taking his cheek in his hand. "Listen to me good and believe it down deep. I want you in every single way. And I will tell you and show you that every day if that's what it takes to make you believe it." Jeremy kissed him once, twice, knowing that his father's lack of acceptance made it so that Charlie was probably going to require a whole lot of reassurance. Jer was only too happy to give it.

Charlie nodded. "Then I would love to move in here with you." His expression went serious. "I just want to say something, Jeremy. Your brother might've saved me, but you're the one who rescued me from a lonely life not worth living. I love you."

"I love you, too. And you'll never be lonely again, Charlie. I promise you that," Jeremy said, pulling him in for another kiss.

"So, when do you want me to move my stuff over here?" Charlie asked.

Jeremy was off the bed like a shot. He threw Charlie's jeans at him while he jumped into his own. The biggest, happiest belly laugh spilled from Charlie's mouth. Jeremy had never heard him laugh so freely before, and it was his new favorite sound. He would fucking live to give Charlie cause to make it again and again.

"Sooo, that would mean now, then?" Charlie asked, sitting up and still wearing a big smile.

"You better believe it," Jeremy said. The team's investigation might be impossibly complicated and their enemies enormously powerful, but no matter what, Jeremy would have the man he loved standing at his side. "I want to make you mine in every way I can, Charlie. And I want to do it right now."

Acknowledgments

ONE OF THE biggest and most wonderful surprises to me about the whole Hard Ink series was how quickly Jeremy Rixey became a favorite character. From the very first book, everyone wanted to know if Jeremy was going to get a story, and I was beyond thrilled to be able to do just that in *Hard to Be Good*! For that opportunity, I first and foremost have to thank all the readers who wanted Jeremy to have his very own happily-ever-after. And then I have to thank my wonderful editor, Amanda Bergeron, for agreeing Jeremy's story needed to be told—and for wholeheartedly embracing with whom he was going to find his happy ending. It's been an amazing experience to work with an editor who so got my vision for this series and who loves the characters as much as I do, so thank you, Amanda!

My next thanks must go to Christi Barth, as always, for reading the book and giving me amazing comments that made it better and better. She's been there beside me throughout the entire series, and I can't thank her enough for helping me make the Hard Ink team shine!

Thanks also to my agent, Kevan Lyon, for diving into this series with me and for helping make Jeremy and Charlie's story come true! And thanks to KP Simmon for being the world's best cheerleader, shoulder to lean on, and (when necessary) conspirator! I'm really lucky to have such an amazing team of women to work with!

From the very first book people were suggesting that if the team was going to have a dog, they needed a cat, too. And, of course, it couldn't be a *normal* cat! Thanks to reader-friend Krystal Boehm for the inspiration for Cy. From the time she posted a picture of Cyrus, her orange one-eyed cat, on Eileen's Facebook page, I knew he'd have to make an appearance in the Hard Ink world. (But, of course, the guys had to twist his name just a little. I hope Cyrus understands!) Oh, and Krystal, *happy birthday!*

I must thank wonderful writer friends Lea Nolan and Stephanie Dray, who are always there for me. And I must thank my Heroes, my wonderful street team, too! You guys rock! Finally, thanks to my family for making it all possible!

As always, thanks to the readers for taking my characters into their hearts and letting them tell their stories again and again.

With my love,
LK

**Want to see the moment Nick unveils
his new tattoo to Becca?
Keep an eye out for news of this
exciting bonus scene at
www.facebook.com/LauraKayeWrites
for details coming soon!**

Don't miss the explosive final chapter
of the Hard Ink series . . .

HARD TO LET GO

Beckett Murda hates to dwell on the past.
But his investigation into the ambush
that killed half his Special Forces team
and ended his Army career gives him
little choice. Just when his team learns
how powerful their enemies are, hard-ass
Beckett encounters his biggest complication
yet—seductive, feisty Katherine Rixey.

A tough, stubborn prosecutor, Kat visits her
brothers' Hard Ink Tattoo shop following a
bad break-up—and finds herself staring down
the barrel of a stranger's gun. Beckett is hard-
bodied and sexy as hell, but he's also the most
infuriating man ever. Worse, Kat's brothers
are at war with the criminals her office is

investigating. When Kat joins the fight, she lands straight in Beckett's sights . . . and in his arms. Not to mention their enemies' crosshairs. Now Beckett and Kat must set aside their differences to work together, because the only thing sweeter than justice is finding love and never letting go.

Coming Summer 2015
Keep reading for a sneak peek!

THE WAREHOUSE WAS an abandoned shell. Empty so long that parts of the roof had caved in, most of the windows were gone, and nature had started to reclaim the concrete and cinder block, with bits of green taking root in the building's cracks. Proof of the resilience of life, even in the worst of circumstances.

Most of Beckett Murda's life was proof of that.

The whistling early morning wind and the distant sounds of Baltimore car traffic and ships' horns were the only noises that made their way into this corner of what was left of the fourth floor, and that was just fine by Beckett. Because the height and the quiet and the seclusion made it the perfect place from which to protect what he cared about most.

His friends.

His brothers.

His chance at redemption.

Crouching beside a busted window gave Beckett the perfect view of Hard Ink Tattoo, his temporary home the past two and a half weeks. Or, at least, it was the perfect place to see what was left of it. The red-brick L-shaped building sat on the opposite corner of the intersection. Just a few days before, the center of the long side of the L had been reduced to rubble, courtesy of his enemies. The predawn attack had claimed the lives of three good men. Three too damn many.

With Wednesday morning daylight just breaking, Beckett scanned a one-eighty from left to right, his gaze sequentially moving from the empty roads that led to Hard Ink's intersection, to Hard Ink itself, to the surrounding buildings—all empty just as this one was except for Hard Ink. Luckily, the side on which their group lived hadn't suffered any loss of integrity during the attack, so they hadn't had to relocate their base of operations.

Beckett repeated the survey using a pair of high-power binoculars, useful for picking up details he might otherwise miss, given the loss of acuity he'd experienced in his right eye from a grenade explosion just over a year ago. His left was 20/20 all the way, but shrapnel had reduced his right to 20/160. His visual impairment in that eye was damn close to legally blind, and it made seeing at a distance a bitch.

That explosion marked the beginning of the whole clusterfuck that led to him sitting in this hellhole all night. Beckett's Army Special Forces team had been ambushed at a checkpoint in Afghanistan, and their commander and six other members of the team had been killed. In addition to himself, the four survivors—his best friend, Derek "Marz" DiMarzio; second-in-command Nick Rixey; Shane McCallan; and Edward "Easy" Cantrell—had fought tooth and nail to make it out alive, only to be blamed for their teammates' deaths, accused of dereliction of duty, and sent packing from the Army courtesy of other-than-honorable discharges and nondisclosure agreements ensuring they could never say anything to try to clear their names.

Now they were doing it anyway. This was their one and only shot.

Movement along the far side of Hard Ink.

Beckett focused in to see Katherine Rixey pause at the corner before running across the road to the shadows of the opposite building. From there, Nick's younger sister skirted tight along the wall, darted across the road again, and then disappeared from view as she entered the warehouse where he hid. Within a minute the rapid thump of footsteps echoed up the stairwell.

Nearly 6:00 a.m., which meant his shift in the sniper's roost was done. Kat was his relief.

Except that was maybe the only way Kat Rixey relieved him. Otherwise, she had an impressive knack for getting way far under his skin and pushing all his buttons. And every one of his teammates had witnessed it firsthand. Among elite operatives, lives and missions depended on being able to recognize and mitigate your weaknesses. And that meant Beckett had to admit that something about Kat distracted him, irritated him, made him . . . feel.

Not something he had much experience with. Not for years.

Her footsteps neared, their sound louder in the stairwell, and Beckett's heart might've kicked up in time with her jogging pace. Something about her threw him off-kilter. And that fucking pissed him off. Because this woman was the younger sister of one of his best friends. And no part of what he was doing here involved—

"Hey, Trigger. You're free to go," she said as she stepped into the large room behind him.

Fucking Trigger. She'd been at him with her cute little nicknames since the day they met. Like it was his fault he'd caught her roaming Hard Ink unannounced and pulled his gun on her. Times being what they were, she was lucky that was all he'd done. He kept his eyes trained out the window so she couldn't see the irritation likely filling his expression.

"Helloooo?" she said, standing right behind him.

Taking his good old time, he put the binoculars down and slowly turned toward her. And had to work hard to keep from reacting to how fucking hot she was.

Katherine Rixey was an angel-faced beauty with a foul mouth, sharp green eyes, and curves that would not quit. His hands nearly ached to bury themselves in her thick, wavy brown hair every time he saw her, and the sight of her confidently and competently handling a gun made him rock hard. The fact that she was apparently a shark of a prosecutor was just icing on her five-foot-two-inch cake. Brains, body, beauty. Kat had it all. Too bad she drove him bat-shit crazy.

She waved a hand in front of his face, and he tore his gaze away. "You fall asleep there, Quick-Draw? Shoulda texted me. I would've come sooner."

Whatever you do, do not *think about her coming*.

Jesus.

Beckett secured his weapon in a holster at his lower

back, hauled himself off the floor, and swallowed the innuendo-filled retorts flitting through his mind. "Had it covered just fine."

"Good to know," she said, crossing her arms and smirking.

Beckett felt his eyebrow arch in question before he'd thought to school his expression. "Problem?" he asked, stepping right up in front of her. She was so short, he towered over her, forcing her to tilt her head back to meet his gaze. And damn if she didn't smell good, like warm, sweet vanilla. It made his mouth water, his groin tighten, and his temper flare. Sonofabitch.

"Dude. I am *so* not the one with the problem." Amusement filled her bright green eyes.

As he nailed her with a stare, Beckett tried not to admire the way her crossed arms lifted the mounds of her breasts under the clingy black long-sleeved tee. This woman was a Rixey, which meant sarcasm was coded into her DNA. Beckett had a decade of experience with her oldest brother to know that was true. No way he was giving her the satisfaction of a reply. He shook his head and stepped around her.

"Always a pleasure," she said.

He peered over his shoulder to find her lowering into a crouch by the window. She grabbed a gun from one of the cases on the floor and checked the weapon's ammo. Her quick motions revealed her confidence and experience— always sexy qualities to Beckett's mind.

Still, despite her obvious competence with a weapon— Nick had done a damn fine job making sure his petite little sister could take care of herself—her being alone up here for a day-long shift didn't sit well in Beckett's gut. Ever since the attack on Hard Ink, everyone who had any experience with weapons had been taking shifts in one of the two lookouts they'd set up, and Katherine had more than earned the right to help with the task. More than that, they needed all hands on deck right now—including Katherine. But the team's enemies were expertly trained, highly lethal mercenaries who had no qualms about covering their asses, no matter what it took—or who they took down. And where Katherine was concerned, that made Beckett . . . worry.

After all, she was Nick's sister. And just like the rest of the team, Nick had lost enough.

And that's all it was. Right.

Sonofabitch.

"Watch yourself," Beckett said, voice gruff.

Katherine peered over her shoulder at him and rolled her eyes. "Yeah, that's kinda the point of this whole thing," she said, gesturing to the guns, ammo, communication devices, Army green sleeping bags, and stack of bottled water and snacks piled around the corner by the window. When Beckett didn't reply, she shook her head and looked outside again. "You question Nick and the guys this way when you hand off your shift?"

No, he didn't. And saying so would either make him look like a chauvinist asshole or possibly reveal too damn much about the shit she stirred up inside him. So he disappeared into the stairwell and made his way down.

Given the strength and resources of their enemies,

sparring with Katherine Rixey was the last thing he needed to waste energy doing.

"THAT'S WHAT I thought," Kat said. Looking back toward the stairs again, she realized she was alone. As big as Beckett freaking Murda was, how the hell did she not hear him leave?

Damn Special Forces guys. Her brother Nick had the same ability. Scared her half to death sometimes. Thank God for their middle brother, Jeremy. Most of the time, Jer gave off a happy vibe you could feel coming from a mile away.

Kat smiled at the thought, settled into a comfortable position, and turned her attention back to the view outside the window. The streets were eerily quiet, which wasn't an accident. Though her brothers had bought a building in the city's derelict and partly abandoned old industrial district, the real explanation behind the ghost town she was looking down on was a series of roadblocks a police ally of Nick's had somehow orchestrated. Kat had tried to stay out of the specifics, because she hadn't wanted to know the details if they potentially veered into the illegal.

Which was damn near a certainty. She had come to visit her brothers at Hard Ink five days before, and pretty much the whole time she'd been here had walked a fine line between wanting to help them with this crazy situation and freaking out about the illegal nature of what they were doing. Not that the guys weren't justified in defending themselves and doing whatever it took to clear their names, but she had become a lawyer for a reason. Growing up, Nick was the risk taker, the guy who ditched college weeks into his senior year to join the Army. Jeremy was the artistic rule breaker. And she had been the rule follower.

Almost like checking a series of boxes, she'd gotten straight A's all through school, served as the president of all her clubs, got into the best colleges and busted her ass to become managing editor of her law review. Even as early as high school, she'd known she wanted to go into the law. Because law represented justice and order and righteousness. Those ideals had spoken to her, drawn her to a career fighting what she thought was the good fight.

Four years into working at the Department of Justice, she still believed that was what she and the good people she worked with tried to do. Problem was, sometimes a big gulf existed between what they tried to do and what the law allowed them to achieve. And she'd never realized just how all-consuming the career would be. Twelve-hour days at her desk were her norm.

Kat surveyed the run-down neighborhood outside the window. Baltimore might've only been about thirty miles from D.C., but right now she felt about a million miles away from that desk.

Down below, the street beside Hard Ink was literally blocked—by the pile of rubble that had slid down into the road when part of the building collapsed early Sunday morning. Just looking at the pile of bricks and cement and twisted beams and broken glass made Kat's heart race, because she'd been on top of that building when it went down. Her brothers and several others, too. In her mind's eye she saw the rooftop fall away from under Jeremy's feet. He and two other guys started to fall, and she'd screamed. And then Nick was there, grabbing Jeremy's hand and hauling him up from the breach.

Kat's breath caught and she blinked away the sting suddenly filling her eyes. The image of Jer falling and the thought of him being gone had haunted her dreams every night since. Because she could've lost Jeremy.

Which made her glad her oldest brother had spent years in SpecOps and knew what the hell to do, because she couldn't lose her brothers. And given the impossibly crazy situations she'd encountered since arriving at Hard Ink, she was well aware that losing them was a possibility. Because Nick and Jeremy were in the very gravest danger.

It all stemmed from Nick's team's fight to restore their honor against powerful and not fully known enemies. A fight that apparently had so much at stake that her brothers' building had been attacked by armed soldiers who had a rocket launcher. *A freaking rocket launcher*!

And, if that wasn't enough, the men they were likely fighting against—and probably the very ones who had attacked—were the subject of a series of investigations her office had been working on for the past nine months.

It was something she'd only become certain of over the last twenty-four hours, as Nick's team's investigation into a cache of documents from their now-deceased Army commander had begun to shed light upon exactly what—and who—they were up against. Kat was glad for the alone time today, because her brain was a conflicted mess. Should she maintain her professional ethics and protect her security clearances by keeping her mouth shut? Or tell Nick and his team exactly what her office was doing and share what information she had that could help them?

She'd promised herself to decide today while she had some time to think.

And she had thought that coming to see her big bros would be the relaxing getaway it normally was, one that would distract her from her own problems—namely Cole, the ex-boyfriend who couldn't seem to get it through his thick skull that she was really done with him.

Down below, she saw Beckett dart across the street between the buildings. With his muscles, square jaw, and fathomless blue eyes, the guy was pure, raw masculinity personified. Her body couldn't be near his without reacting on some fundamentally hormonal level. Her heart raced. Her nipples peaked. Her stomach went for a loop-the-loop.

Before he disappeared around the corner of the Hard Ink building, he glanced over his shoulder and looked up. Kat was a hundred percent sure his eyes landed on her, even though she sat mostly shielded behind the brick of this old warehouse. Because her body jangled with a sudden awareness.

And then he was gone.

She rolled her eyes. Freaking ridiculous to get so worked up over a man whose favorite form of communication was the grunt. And who made a habit of ignoring her when she spoke to him. And who'd pulled a gun on her without even bothering to ask her name. Couldn't forget that.

Whatever. He probably just got to her because he was so unlike the men with whom she normally spent time. Whereas her colleagues at Justice tended to be serious, buttoned-up, and lower key, Beckett radiated an intensity she didn't quite understand. It certainly didn't have anything to do with how he spoke or acted, because he talked little and showed emotion even less. Maybe it was all that leashed strength, because she had no doubt that he could do some serious damage with his bare hands.

Which, given the way her biceps looked right now, maybe wasn't the most pleasant thought, was it? Because Friday morning, when she'd gone down to her building's garage to head out to work, Cole had been waiting for her . . . somewhere. One minute she was juggling her belongings and sliding her key into the door lock, and the next someone grabbed her arms from behind and shoved her against the cold cinder-block wall near the hood of her car. It caught her so off guard that she hadn't even managed a scream before her body was trapped between the wall and her assailant, who ground his hard-on into her rear.

God, I missed you, baby.

The memory of his raspy voice whispering in her ear made her shudder. The fact that he'd gotten the jump on her without her having the chance to fight back had Kat so mad at herself she could barely stand it.

When she'd finally talked him into letting go of her

and agreed to meet him after work for a drink and a talk, he left. And she'd hightailed it up to her apartment to pack a bag, made a stop at the Superior Court to file for a protective order, and left D.C. for Baltimore and the safety of her brothers' place.

Ha.

So much for that.

But at least she knew Cole wasn't going to be a problem here. She'd received a message yesterday that the judge had granted the order, and once the authorities served Cole with the papers putting the order into effect, he'd keep his distance. He was too damn smart and appearance-conscious not to. And, as an attorney, he'd obviously realize that getting caught violating a protective order would create problems with the bar in addition to problems with the police.

Kat couldn't wait for the order to be served. Not only would it give her peace of mind that he'd stay away, but the no-contact provision should also cut off the stream of demanding and accusatory texts and voice mails she'd received since she pulled a no-show for their talk Friday night. Couldn't happen soon enough.

Given everything that was going on with her brothers, the knowledge that the order would diffuse the Cole situation allowed Kat to breathe a sigh of relief. Because they really couldn't handle even one more complication.

About the Author

LAURA KAYE IS the *New York Times* and *USA Today* bestselling author of more than a twenty books in contemporary and paranormal romance and romantic suspense. Laura grew up amid family lore involving angels, ghosts, and evil-eye curses, cementing her lifelong fascination with storytelling and the supernatural. Laura lives in Maryland with her husband, two daughters, and cute-but-bad dog, and appreciates her view of the Chesapeake Bay every day.

Discover great authors, exclusive offers, and more at hc.com.